RAVEN

A CREEPY HOLLOW STORY

Also by Rachel Morgan

THE CREEPY HOLLOW SERIES

The Faerie Guardian

The Faerie Prince

The Faerie War

A Faerie's Secret

A Faerie's Revenge

A Faerie's Curse

Glass Faerie

Shadow Faerie

Rebel Faerie

CREEPY HOLLOW
COMPANION STORIES

Scarlett

Raven

RAVEN

A CREEPY HOLLOW STORY

RACHEL MORGAN

RACHEL
MORGAN

This story takes place approximately twenty years before *The Faerie Guardian* (Creepy Hollow, Book One).

CHAPTER ONE

THE MAGICALLY ENHANCED SPOTLIGHT BURNED RAVEN'S eyes as she crossed the stage and stopped at its center to face the vast auditorium. With her heart thumping in her chest, she placed one hand on her hip and sashayed the length of the runway. Her starlight blue dress hugged her body all the way down to her knees, where it flared out in a train made of thousands of tiny jewels glittering with enchanted light. As she neared the end of the runway, the wings that encased her shoulders and upper arms slowly began to unfurl.

She stopped and struck a pose—and in that instant, the lower edge of her dress caught alight. The flames blazed blue, exactly as she'd planned, encircling her in a ring of brilliant light. What she hadn't planned, however, were the flames that leaped up and ignited the tips of her silver gloves. Nor the

1

whoosh of heat and light at her back that most likely meant her delicate spider-thread wings had caught fire. A flare of heat near her neck alerted her to the fact that the spherical lattice-work around her head was next. Considering the spells she'd already placed upon the headpiece, adding flames to the mix was *not* a good idea.

Having extinguished her burning gloves with a quick water spell, Raven grabbed the cage-like structure, tugged it open, and pulled it off her head. It had already caught alight, and as she tossed it away, the entire thing exploded. She shrieked and ducked down, shielding her face from the glare and falling debris.

The flames flickered away.

Silence settled over the auditorium.

The enchanted spotlight dimmed.

Raven lowered her arms, straightened, and looked out across the empty rows of chairs until her eyes fell upon the lone figure in the back row. Vera Drizwold, director of the Delphinium College of Fashion and Design, sat with her arms folded tightly across her chest. Slowly, she lifted the clipboard from her lap and stood. "I'm afraid I can't approve this one, Raven. As lovely as the design is, it's far too dangerous. I like your incorporation of star-fire, but it's extremely unstable. You won't stand a chance of winning the show if you wind up killing the poor model wearing your creation, blowing up half the audience, and damaging the building." Her gaze fell upon the rubble that had fallen to the floor just in front of the runway. "You'll need to clean that up. Make sure it's done before the weekend. We're using this hall on Saturday."

She left the room, her ever-present clipboard soaring obediently through the air behind her.

Refusing to curse out loud with frustration, Raven pulled the delicate wings—fashioned after sprite wings—back down over her shoulders before climbing carefully off the runway. She might not be allowed to use this dress for her final show, but she didn't want to ruin what was left of it. She'd worked too hard to give it up completely. She bent to retrieve the few remaining bits of the headpiece, strands of dark brown and magenta hair falling in her face. As she straightened, footsteps echoed through the auditorium.

"I'm so sorry." Daisy, her oldest friend, walked up to her. "I know how badly you wanted it to work."

"You saw what happened?"

"Yes. I was peeking through the door back there." Daisy nodded her blonde and blue head toward the door Director Drizwold had left through. "Why didn't it work this time?"

"I don't know," Raven muttered. "You've seen me practicing in this outfit. All the flame spells worked perfectly together. Nothing blew up. But of course, when the director was here, everything went wrong."

"At least you hadn't finished all the detailing on the dress yet. Imagine how much more time you would have lost."

"Still a number of hours of wasted work. And I so badly wanted this dress to be the one. The outfit that beats everyone's expectations. How am I going to impress Mella Cascata if I don't produce something spectacular? I need to wow her." Raven frowned at the pieces of metal in her hands. "It must have been the flame retardant spell that didn't work. I can fix that. Maybe I should just go ahead with this design anyway. I *know* I can make it work."

"And if you don't?" Daisy said carefully. "Is it worth landing yourself a reputation as a pyromaniac?"

Raven let out a long sigh that was almost a groan. "I don't know. Sometimes you have to take risks if you want to get anywhere. And if I don't do something amazing, I'll never win the show."

Daisy patted Raven's arm. "Have I told you before that I'm so glad I don't have to compete against you?"

"Yes. And I agree. It would suck having to try to beat my best friend."

"And there's the fact that I wouldn't have a clue what to do with clothes," Daisy added. "Give me furniture and curtains any day."

Raven managed a chuckle at that. "Absolutely *thrilling* stuff."

"It totally is. Anyway, I need to get going, and you need to change."

"Yeah. I'll clean up the rest of this mess tomorrow."

Backstage, Raven changed out of her disaster of a dress and back into her three-quarter pants, billowing white shirt cinched at the waist with a bright pink belt, and the heels she'd spent an hour this morning morphing into lightning bolt shapes. She placed the sprite-wing dress carefully inside a garment bag so she could take it home. She wouldn't be needing it at college anymore.

Despite her failure, Raven held her head high as she tugged open the auditorium door. No one else needed to know how badly she'd messed up her demo with the director. Her spirits lifted a little as she left the dim hall behind and walked into the bright afternoon light of the hallways. Even after five years, she still felt a bit of a thrill walking through the illustrious Delphinium College of Fashion and Design. Started by top fashion designer Mella Cascata before she stepped back and handed the reigns to someone else, it was a small, prestigious college, open only to the most talented of students—and those whose parents could afford a hefty donation. Raven hoped she fell into the first category, though she'd never had the guts to ask her parents.

She descended the polished marble stairway outside and waited in the front garden, just inside the main gate. On any other day, she would have headed home on her own through the faerie paths, but on Thursdays her mother finished lunch with the ladies twenty minutes before Delph classes ended, so she always stopped by to pick Raven up. Raven had never wanted to be one of those students who was transported home in an ostentatious carriage pulled by pegasi, but she'd decided not to tell her mother that. She figured she could handle it once a week.

As students all around her wrote faerie paths spells with their styluses onto any available surface—the pillars by the gate, the ground, the oversized statue of Mella Cascata at the center of the garden—she crossed her arms and watched them. The surfaces seemed to pull away wherever a spell was written, revealing the utter darkness of the faerie paths beyond. Students walked in and vanished, along with the temporary doorways. With her feet beginning to hurt in the lightning bolt shoes—she'd probably made them a little too high—Raven sat on the edge of the statue's pedestal and looked around. The college rose behind her, grand and beautiful in its design, with tall, slender trees surrounding the property for miles. It was a beautiful setting to work in every day.

She removed her amber from her bag and checked its smooth surface for messages. Nothing from her mother, so she dropped the rectangular slab back into her bag. Just then, her parents' carriage rolled to a stop outside the main gate. Raven stood and walked toward it, her pink tote bag over her shoulder and her sprite-wing dress trailing through the air behind her in its garment bag. She handed it to the driver.

"How did it go?" her mother asked as Raven climbed into the carriage. Zalea always greeted Raven this way, with a question about her latest project or assessment. Never 'hello' or 'how was your day?'.

"Not that well," Raven replied, sitting on the cushioned seat across from her mother and lowering her tote bag to the floor. The cloying scent of perfume made her want to cough. She shifted closer to the window, pushed the curtain aside, and touched her fingertips to the clear surface. It vanished a moment later, and as the carriage began to move, fresh air slipped inside.

"What do you mean? Didn't the director like your piece?"

"She did, but I had a bit of a problem with the pyrotechnic spells. She decided this outfit is too dangerous."

"Too *dangerous*?" Zalea repeated, her tone suggesting this was an absurd concept.

"There may have been a small explosion."

"Oh." Zalea sighed and leaned back, folding her hands in

her lap. "This isn't like you, Raven. You know we expect the very best of you."

"Yes, thank you, Mom." Raven tucked one leg beneath her, which was quite an accomplishment considering the size and shape of her heel. "I'm aware of all the things you *expect* of me."

"Please don't use that tone with me. And take your foot off the seat. You'll make it dirty."

"Jeez, Mom, my shoes are clean. I made them this morning."

"There's no such thing as clean shoes."

Making a show of rolling her eyes—because she knew how much Zalea loved that—Raven returned her foot to the floor. "I'm going to invent a spell that makes shoes perpetually clean."

"I doubt that will win the show for you, Raven, so you'd better come up with something equally as dazzling as the sprite dress." She waved her hand at the door, and the glass reappeared in the window. "And *not* something that's going to explode all over everyone. We don't want the family name brought down by an embarrassment like that."

"I know, I know." Raven turned her attention to the view outside as the carriage rose into the air. She'd heard her mother's concerns about The Family Name far too many times for it to bother her anymore. Personally, she didn't give a pixie's ass about The Family Name. All she cared about was making a successful career in fashion, and that meant winning the final show and landing herself an internship at the House of Cascata.

Darkness gathered around the carriage, blotting out the view as the faerie paths surrounded them. Raven always wondered how the driver managed to open such a large doorway to the paths while simultaneously directing the pegasi, but she'd never had the opportunity to ask him. Seconds later, light appeared once more, and the carriage sailed into the air near Raven's home.

"Oh, that other showcase I was invited to be part of is next week," she said, turning to her mother as she remembered the Von Milta Madness event. "Will you and Dad come?"

Zalea frowned. "What showcase? Have you mentioned it before?"

"Yes, more than once. Von Milta Madness. It happens every year."

"It doesn't have anything to do with Delphinium or your final show, does it?"

Raven fidgeted with the edge of the curtain. "No."

"Are you sure you should be taking part? All your time should now be dedicated to—"

"The work is already done, Mom. I've sent in my pieces. I just thought you and Dad might want to come along."

"Oh. Well if it doesn't have anything to do with the final show, I'm not sure your father will have time. I think he has meetings lined up every night next week. Oh, and you and I are hosting the annual flower casters' party next Friday, remember?"

Raven nodded, her expression remaining neutral. She would have been surprised if Zalea's answer to the showcase invitation had been yes. Still, Raven always asked. Just in case.

The carriage wheels struck the ground, rocking her forward and then back again as it continued smoothly forward. "How was lunch with the ladies?" she asked politely as her fingers rubbed the creases of fabric in her shirt.

Zalea patted her short, well-styled hair, making sure not a single black or orange strand was out of place. "It was nice enough. That ill-behaved waitress has been fired, so Marigold was happy. And Lucida said she loves the dress design you drew for her. She's thinking about having it made up for Crispin's first century birthday party next month, so that will be wonderful exposure for you. Oh, and her son Orson has returned from his year of traveling. You remember him, don't you?"

Raven's hands stilled in her lap. Unease curled in her stomach. "Yes, I remember him."

"He joined us for lunch. Told us all about his adventures. Fascinating, really."

Raven picked her pink bag up and hugged it to her chest. Why was the carriage taking so long to come to a stop? Surely their driveway wasn't normally this long. She cleared her throat. "Um, is that allowed? I thought ladies' lunches were for ladies."

"Yes, but we can make an exception for a nice young man like Orson Willowstack," her mother said with a smile. "And," she added with a half-smile, "he's just the right age for you."

"Seriously, Mom?"

"Of course I'm serious. He's the perfect match for you, Raven, and very handsome. You told me so yourself when you first met him."

He most certainly was not the perfect match for Raven. "And how old was I back then? Twelve? I might have a very different opinion now."

"You won't," Zalea assured her. "He's just as charming as ever, and he's joining his father's stylus manufacturing business soon. He would be able to provide wonderfully well for you while you indulge your creative side."

"Thanks, Mom. I haven't even left school and you're already planning my union."

"Well someone has to take care of you when it's no longer your father's job."

There were so many things wrong with that statement that Raven didn't bother responding.

"Anyway, he'll be at the Harlington Home fundraiser on Monday night. The two of you can catch up."

"Wonderful," Raven said, knowing her sarcasm would go right over Zalea's head.

The carriage finally, *finally* circled the teardrop shape at the end of the driveway and came to a halt. Raven climbed out quickly. The average faerie home was concealed by glamour magic within a tree, but there was nothing average about her parents' home. It was built right out in the open and was probably large enough to house a small village. She'd been told that the glamour spells required to conceal homes of this size were too complex for something as small and simple as a tree. While that might be true, Raven suspected it had more to do with the upper class's desire to show off their ostentatious homes than anything else.

After collecting her garment bag, Raven walked up to the

front door with Zalea at her side. A young man stood guard at the door next to an exotic arrangement of flowers in a tall pot. Raven smiled at him as she passed, and he returned her greeting with a nod before looking out across the grounds again.

Zalea waited for the door to close behind them before speaking. "Raven," she said, her disapproving tone hinting at the warning beneath.

"I'm just being polite, Mom."

"It isn't appropriate."

"It isn't appropriate to be polite?" Raven repeated, though she knew that wasn't what Zalea meant.

"It has nothing to do with manners, and you know it. It isn't appropriate because he's here to guard our home, not to interact with us."

"He's a *person*, Mom. And I'm not so superior that I can walk past him and pretend he doesn't exist."

"But you are superior, darling." Zalea removed her scarf and draped it over her arm. "He's just a guard. You're practically royalty."

Raven choked out a laugh. "Oh my goodness, Mom. There is no world in which we are even close to being royalty. Wealth does not equal nobility."

"Perhaps not, but it's essentially the same thing to a person like him. It sets you so far above him that you may as well be a princess."

With a groan of exasperation, Raven headed for the stairs. "I can't believe I'm related to someone so narrow-minded and snobby."

"I'm going to pretend I didn't hear you being so rude," Zalea called back to Raven as she crossed the entrance hall.

Raven reached her bedroom, a large semicircular space near the top of a small tower, and dumped her pink bag just inside the door. She sent her dress soaring toward the walk-in closet while stepping out of her shoes. Instead of aiming for the bed or the overly curvy couch or the desk above which an enchanted number fifteen floated, Raven sat down in the middle of her floor. Aside from the soft carpet she enjoyed running her fingers over, there was something about sitting cross-legged on the floor that helped her think. Things just seemed easier down here.

A wave of her hand brought her college bag closer, along with a pile of notebooks from her desk. She spread the books around her, picked one at random, and began paging through past sketches. She read the scribbles of ideas other students had written down during group brainstorming sessions, and the occasional note of feedback from one of the teachers. There must be something in here she could work with.

But nothing spoke to her like the sprite-wing dress, and eventually she tossed the notebooks aside and leaned back on her hands. She stared at the glowing blue fifteen floating above her desk. Fifteen days until the final show. Fifteen days in which to come up with an incredible new dress design, make the actual dress, weave in all the appropriate magic, fit it to the model, test it, and make final adjustments. All while finishing up the remainder of her coursework.

"I can do this," she murmured to herself. Then she grabbed

her latest notebook, turned to a blank page, and sketched out ideas until dinner time.

Dinner was extra long. Her mother wouldn't keep quiet about the flower casters' party she was organizing for the following Friday, and her father, who'd attended a meeting held in the human realm, went on and on—for possibly the hundredth time—about how faeries should consider a magical alternative to television.

Finally, back inside her bedroom, Raven pulled a backpack from beneath her bed. After securing it to her back, she pushed aside her richly embroidered curtains and walked onto the balcony. She turned and looked up at the turret above her room. Carefully, she climbed onto the balustrade, inserted her fingers into the gaps between the wall's outer stones, and began pulling herself up the short distance to the top. She swung her legs over the parapet and looked across the tower at the guard standing on the other side. The guard she'd smiled at earlier.

"Hey," he said, turning to face her with a lunchbox in his hand. "I was starting to think you weren't coming tonight."

CHAPTER TWO

"SORRY," RAVEN SAID AS SHE HURRIED ACROSS THE CIRCULAR space toward Flint. "Dinner took longer than usual. I kept thinking about you waiting up here, wasting your break, but my mother just wouldn't shut up."

"Ah, yes, dinner with the royals." Flint nodded, then took a bite of his sandwich.

Raven's eyebrows pulled together. "The royals?"

He chewed, then said, "You're practically royalty, right?"

Mortification heated her skin as she realized what Flint was referring to. "You heard that?"

"I was on the other side of the door. Neither of you were speaking quietly."

"Ugh, I'm so sorry." Raven covered her face with her hands. "I can't stand how elitist my mother is. It's so embarrassing."

With an easy laugh, Flint shrugged and looked up at the cloud of tiny glow-bugs floating above the tower. "She isn't the first person to think I'm beneath her. I doubt she'll be the last. Fortunately," he added as he set his lunchbox aside, "she was unsuccessful in passing on her elitist ways to her one and only daughter."

"Yes, to her ongoing disappointment." Raven removed a bowl from her backpack and placed it at the center of the tower. "Now she's trying to set me up with the son of one of her equally elitist friends."

"Oh?" Flint, who was kneeling beside her backpack removing the bottle of yuro leaf extract, looked up with a frown.

"Mm hm. Stuck-up guy I have less than zero interest in, which means my mother will soon have more reason to be disappointed in me."

"Oh." Flint returned his attention to the backpack before Raven could see his expression. He took the bottle of yuro leaf extract and poured it into the bowl. As he picked it up and carefully swirled it, Raven raised her hand toward the glow-bugs, a rare, miniature variety known as lavagems, and began to speak the collecting spell while moving her hand in the correct patterns. The spell would trap the glow-bugs' light in liquid form in the bowl, and after standing beneath the moon for six hours, the remaining liquid could be used in various types of magic, including some of the design and clothes casting spells Raven liked to play with.

Once Flint had got the bowl's contents swirling on its own and Raven had finished the incantation, the two of them stood back and stared up at the glittering, star-filled sky. The glow-bug swarm continued to hang just above the tower, the individual bugs moving in slow, lazy patterns. An owl hooted nearby, and the distant trickle of water from the river that ran through the garden reached their ears.

"I'm not complaining about helping you," Flint said after a minute or two, "but surely you must have enough lavagem light by now?"

"What do you mean 'enough'?" She laughed and bumped him playfully with her elbow. "You know I'll only get about a thimble-full tonight."

"Which you told me—the first night we met—was enough for plenty of magic."

"And I thought it was, but I've since come up with so many different ways to use it. It's such a fascinating and versatile element. And since I have a free source of it right here, I don't have to hold back when using it, because I can get more every week." She didn't add that she liked Flint's company and this was an easy excuse to spend time with him.

"Well I'm happy to continue helping you," he said as the two of them moved to the edge of the turret and sat down, "so that no one thinks you're a burglar."

"You were the only one who thought I was a burglar." She chuckled at the memory of the night they'd met, almost a year ago. It was Flint's first night on duty at her parents' home, and Raven's first time collecting lavagem light. She'd bought it several times before, in crystal vials from high-end suppliers. But her allowance didn't always extend that far, and she hated to ask her parents for more. So when she discovered the swarm that liked to hang out above her bedroom at night, she did everything she could to locate the spell to collect their glow. The spell that was best performed by two people, not one.

After managing to convince Flint that she wasn't an intruder but one of the people he'd been hired to protect, he offered to help Raven with her spell. He'd been helping her ever since. They met on top of the tower every week. Originally it was only to set up the lavagem spell, but somehow their meetings continued even when her supply hadn't been depleted, or the tiny bugs disappeared for a while, or the moon was hidden or in the wrong phase.

"How did the demo go today?" Flint asked, then took another bite of his sandwich. Though his question was the same as her mother's, it felt completely different. Nothing but a positive answer was good enough for Zalea, but Flint always seemed interested either way.

"Total disaster," Raven said. "I almost blew up the director."

Flint half choked as he laughed around his sandwich. "Wish I'd been there to see that."

"She said my design is too dangerous. I'm going to have to scrap the whole idea and start again. The final show's only fifteen days away now, and if I don't produce something absolutely show-stopping, my collection won't be good enough to win."

"You know," Flint said carefully, "that it actually won't be the end of the world if you don't win."

"It'll be the end of *my* world," she corrected. "Not because I want to be the best, but because I need that internship. I have no future in fashion if I don't get it."

"Of course you have a future. You're good enough to do this on your own."

His words made her insides leap and her neck and ears heat up. "Well, thank you, but you know it's all about the name. Everyone knows Cascata; nobody knows me. I need to work with a name that's recognizable before I can launch my own."

Flint gave her a pointed look. "Weren't you born with a recognizable name?"

Raven rolled her eyes. "A name that means nothing in fashion."

"But with your talent, your name would soon be known."

The blush crawled further up her neck, making its way to her cheeks. "How do you know anything about my talent?" she asked, a teasing tone to her voice.

"Oh, well … I just mean that you always look good. So, um, you must know how to make good clothes."

Raven looked away as she laughed. "That isn't the half of it, but thank you."

Flint held out his lunchbox to her. "Want some?"

"Of course." She wasn't exactly hungry, but she always enjoyed tasting whatever Flint's mother had packed for him. "Your mom makes the best sandwiches in the world."

"I thought Aunty Sweetpea downstairs was the best cook ever."

"That's what Mom likes to say. And perhaps if Aunty Sweetpea made sandwiches, they would be the best sandwiches in the world, but do you think Zalea Rosewood would allow something as ordinary as a sandwich to grace her dining room table?"

"Hmm. I think I'm gonna go with 'no' on that one."

"Exactly." Raven munched on her sandwich a while. "So, Creepy Hollow, right? That's where you live?"

"Yes. Why?"

"I heard someone mention it earlier while I was waiting to do my demo for the director. Something about a group of reptiscillas attacking a group of elves."

"Oh, yeah. I have a friend at the Creepy Hollow Guild who was involved in breaking up that fight. Things got quite messy."

"Is it scary living there? Things like that happen quite often, don't they?" The thickly forested area known as Creepy Hollow was a good distance away from Raven's home, and she remembered her mother referring to it as a place she hoped never to set foot in.

Flint shrugged. "It isn't as bad as whatever your parents have probably told you. You just have to be careful, that's all. It's actually a beautiful place, if you can look past the potential dangers."

"So you like it there?"

"Yes. Well, it's my home. I haven't thought about living anywhere else."

Raven nodded, though she couldn't identify with that. She'd often thought about what it would be like to live somewhere else one day. "I assume you'll move out of your mom's house at some point, though."

"Why?" He grinned at her. "Do you think I'm too old to be living at home at the age of twenty-two?"

"No, no, I didn't mean that." Her cheeks flushed as she fixed her gaze firmly down at the remainder of her sandwich. "I guess I just can't imagine myself still living at home at that age. Not because I'll be too old, but because I want to put a bit more distance between me and my stuffy parents. But if you have a nice family—and it sounds like you do—then there's nothing wrong with living with them for a bit longer."

Flint tilted his head back against the stones. "I've got centuries ahead of me to live wherever I want. May as well spend another few years at home with my mother and sister. Well," he added with a frown, "I *hope* I have centuries ahead of me, but nothing's guaranteed, of course."

"Yeah, the life of a guardian isn't exactly a safe one," Raven said quietly, thinking of Flint's dad. He'd been a guardian too, but he was killed about five years earlier when he managed to get in the way of some seriously destructive magic. She ate the last bite of her sandwich, lost in thoughts of what a dangerous life Flint must have led before coming to work here.

"My break's almost over," he said after checking the time on his amber. "I'd better get back downstairs."

"Okay." As he stood, Raven pushed herself to her feet along with him. "Thanks for your help."

He smiled. "Any time. Sleep tight, Raven."

As he walked away across the tower, she wrapped her arms around herself and watched the glow-bug cloud.

"Raven?" She met Flint's gaze as he turned back to look at her. "Don't stress about having to come up with a whole new outfit. Whatever you end up making will be incredible."

CHAPTER THREE

"YOU'RE STARTING AGAIN?" POE ASKED.

"Just the last outfit," Raven told him. It was the following afternoon, and she was buried beneath clouds of cerulean tulle in one of the college classrooms. Golden light filtered through the tall, arched windows, lighting up the rows of wide, spacious desks. Most desks were littered with a variety of fabrics, decorative materials, spell ingredients, and unfinished projects. Most of the occupants, however—Raven's fellow senior classmates— had gone home already.

Raven swatted at the bunched up tulle threatening to engulf her and searched the desk surface for her stylus. Glitter stuck to her skin, and feathers poked from her hair. She'd burrowed her way through several supply rooms during lunch, searching for inspiration. It hadn't yet struck, but she needed to get started on *something*.

Poe crossed an arm over his chest, tilted his head to the side, and twisted one of the many piercings in his right ear. "I get that the color matches the rest of your collection, but I'm not sure about the tulle."

"I'm not sure about it either," Raven muttered, leaning over the piece of tulle she was experimenting on and running her stylus across the edge. "How's your collection going? What did the director say about the spinning top hat?"

"Mm, she liked it," Poe said with a shrug. "I think. As long as I can keep it from spinning off the model's head. The craftsmanship of the hat itself is 'commendable—'" he made quotes in the air with his fingers "—but the spell requires improvement."

"She certainly liked it more than the explosion Raven showed her yesterday afternoon," Bella said from across the classroom as she finished tidying her desk and stood up. She dropped her amber into her Rudolpho & Foxx bag and turned to face Raven. "We're all thrilled that you're no longer in the running for the internship."

"Speak for yourself," Poe said, flashing a glare in her direction.

In level tones, Raven said, "You don't think I can pull together something amazing in only two weeks?"

Bella laughed. "Not even the favored Raven Rosewood can do that." She placed her bag on her arm and stepped away from her desk. "Well, unless your daddy buys the winning spot for you."

Without a word, Raven continued running her stylus along

the edge of the tulle, watching it expand and balloon into odd shapes. Most of the students at Delphinium were pleasant—or at least polite enough to keep any gossip about their classmates to a whisper—but Bella had always had an obnoxiously loud mouth. She liked to tell people that her parents had never made a single donation to the college, which must mean she was one of the few students who hadn't bought her way in.

"Don't you have somewhere to be, Bella*donna*," Poe snapped. "A hair stylist, perhaps? Your turquoise locks are looking particularly shabby these days."

Bella stalked from the room without another word.

"I don't see the director asking to see any of *her* pieces," Poe added, jerking his head at the door through which Bella had just left. "So I'm not sure why Miss Belladonna thinks she has any chance of winning the internship."

"You know the director views only some of the pieces prior to the show," Raven said quietly. "Mainly the outfits and spells the teachers have warned her might *not* be appropriate."

"And often," Poe said, turning back to Raven with a flick of his well-styled hair, "the winning collection contains one of those pieces, which means you and I definitely still stand a chance." He draped himself across the least messy part of her desk and sighed. "Although, if I'm honest, I'm a little bit scared of winning. It would be a dream come true to work with Mella Cascata for creative reasons, but everyone says she's such a horrible person."

"Not *everyone*. Perhaps it's only the people who've managed to annoy her that say she's awful."

"Well, a great many people must have annoyed her then.

You know everyone thought for years that she didn't have a family? And then it turned out she just doesn't ever have anything to do with them."

Raven lowered the fabric and looked at Poe. "You know I work in the same industry as you, right? I've heard every story you've heard."

"Have you heard the one about her being related to the Unseelie royal family?"

"Yes. And just like most of the other wild stories out there, it probably isn't true."

"I suppose not." Poe pushed himself up. "Anyway, are you planning to stay late tonight? Do you need some company?"

"Oh, no, don't worry. Being alone helps me think properly." And she didn't mind staying late. It was better than eating dinner with her parents.

"Okay. Try not to stay *too* late. It is Friday, after all."

"Mm hm." Raven returned her attention to the tulle, and by the time Daisy came hurrying in half an hour later, Raven had created a puffed-up mess that left her feeling completely uninspired.

"Hey there," Daisy said, stopping in front of Raven's desk. "How's it going with—Oh. That looks very … high fashion?"

Raven slumped back in her chair. "That's one way of putting it."

"I'm sure you'll come up with something spectacular. You always do."

"Mm." Raven chewed on her thumbnail, then dropped her hand when she remembered how much her mother disapproved of ragged fingernails.

"You know everyone else has gone home, right?" Daisy said.

"Yes. I decided to stay late. I need to get this dress started, and you know I can't work properly at home with my mother fussing about all the mess I'm making. Even when it's in my own bedroom, she starts turning red if I don't keep my desk tidy and put all my materials and equipment away every night. It's so—"

"—creativity stifling. I know. You might have mentioned this before."

"Sorry," Raven said with a small smile.

"Well, I hope inspiration strikes."

"Yeah, me too. Night. Oh, Daisy, wait," she added as her friend turned to leave. "I need to tell you something. It's, uh ..."

"It's what?" Daisy leaned on the desk.

"My mother told me yesterday that ... well ..." Raven swallowed. "Orson is back."

"Oh." Daisy straightened slowly. "Okay."

"He's going to be at the fundraiser on Monday night." Raven closed her eyes for a moment and sighed. "And my mother is hoping to set me up with him."

"I see."

Raven opened her eyes and leaned forward. "She doesn't know anything about what happened before."

"I know." She hesitated. "But do you think *he* will say something?"

Raven shook her head. "He has a reputation to protect, doesn't he?"

"I don't know if that ever mattered much to him. He always did whatever he wanted."

"Daisy, you—"

"I'm not going to make a scene," Daisy said, "as much as I might want to. He isn't worth it."

"No. He definitely isn't." Raven would have to keep reminding herself of that, otherwise she might be the one to make a scene if Orson didn't watch himself. "So everything's going to be fine on Monday night then?" she asked.

"Yes. I mean, do you think it will be fine?"

"Of course. You'll come and get ready at my house? You said you wanted to wear the blue dress I designed for last month's Cast Till You Drop."

"Yes. Thank you." Daisy gave her an awkward wave and walked out. Raven dropped back into her chair with a sigh. Stupid Orson Willowstack. Why couldn't he just stay away? He was so ... so ...

She stared unseeingly at her desk for several moments as images, colors and spells—the spark of an idea she'd been waiting for all day—began ticking through her mind. She bunched up the tulle and tossed it aside, then fished in her bag for a pair of sound drops. After sticking one coin-shaped piece to each temple, she waved her hand past one of them. Music filled her ears. Then she reached for her notebook, turned to a blank page, and began sketching.

Orson was deceitful like a snake, but snakes were also beautiful, mesmerizing, and she'd never used a snake concept before. It would fit in well with the various creatures she'd used as inspiration for her other pieces. She could craft it from silver with glowing flecks of blue the same shade as the rest of her collection. And blue gems for the eyes. The right combination of spells would cause the metallic snake to slither all the way up the model's back, then maybe around her neck and all the way down her back again. Perhaps ending as a belt around her waist. The rest of the dress would need to incorporate the snake concept somehow, but Raven couldn't yet see the specifics in her mind.

She was in the middle of scribbling down every idea that came to mind when a high-pitched squeak reached her over the sound of her music. She ended the sound drop spell with a quick wave and dug around in her bag until she found the decorative round hand mirror responsible for the annoying squeak. Her mother's face appeared in the mirror's glossy surface. With a sigh, Raven leaned back and tapped the screen.

"Where are you?" Zalea demanded before Raven could say a word. "I've just been informed that you're not home yet."

"I'm at Delph working on my replacement for the sprite dress," Raven said. "I sent you a message earlier, remember? You said it was fine."

"Yes, but it's after nine now. That's far too late for you still to be at college. Now you'll have to return home in the dark."

Raven hadn't realized so much time had passed, but that didn't change the fact that Zalea's logic made little sense. "Mom, it would have been dark if I'd left an hour ago. Why is it more of a problem now than it would have been earlier?"

Zalea clicked her tongue in irritation. "Because suspicious characters like to come out when it's late. Suspicious characters who might want to kidnap you for ransom."

Raven couldn't help laughing. "Nobody wants to kidnap me, Mom. Don't be so silly. All I have to do is walk out the front door, write a faerie paths spell, and I'll be inside our home seconds later. You can wait in the entrance hall and see for yourself."

"Your father and I aren't home right now."

"Oh." She wondered what event she'd forgotten about this time. "Well, anyway, I'm finally getting somewhere with this new idea. I just need another half hour or so to get all my ideas down on paper. And I haven't finished cleaning up the explosion mess from—"

"I'm sending a message for a guard to come get you now," Zalea said.

"You really don't need to do that, Mom."

Zalea looked over her shoulder for a moment, as if distracted by something. She laughed, then turned back to Raven. "Wait inside the main entrance. Don't go outside."

"Mom!"

"I'll tell the guard to be there within ten minutes." Zalea's face vanished from the mirror.

Raven groaned and smacked the mirror down onto her desk. Then she shoved it into her bag, grabbed her stylus, amber and jacket—three-quarter sleeves, light-weight, in a bold floral print Daisy had helped her with—and hurried out of the classroom without so much as pushing her chair in. Her desk was messier than anyone else's, but her teachers were used to that by now. As long as her untidiness didn't spill onto anyone else's desk, no one really cared.

She dashed into the auditorium, left her bag on the end of the runway, and cleaned up the remaining rubble with a few quick spells. She should have done it during lunch, but she was too busy hunting down inspiration in the supply rooms. Looking up, she saw a hole in the ceiling leading to the space above where lighting and special effects enchantments were controlled. Was she supposed to fix that too? She wasn't quite sure how, so she'd have to ask Director Drizwold about it tomorrow. "Almost done," she muttered to herself, noticing one last item out of place—a scrap of paper on the runway. She scrambled up in her chunky, square-heeled boots and retrieved the paper, which turned out to be covered in someone else's handwriting, not her own. She stuffed it into her jacket pocket, retrieved her bag, and swung herself down off the runway.

She was about to leave when a sparkle in the first row caught her eye. Looking closer, she discovered a shoe with petal-like pieces that extended upward to around ankle height. It was covered in silver sequins, which blinked in the auditorium's light. She picked up the shoe, admiring the design and wondering who it belonged to. Probably some other student who'd had to get their outfit approved by the director. Someone who was now freaking out about their missing shoe. Raven placed it inside her bag. She would hand it in the next morning.

She walked quickly along the dim hallways, hoping her parents' guard wasn't already waiting. When an echo sounded behind her, she threw a look over her shoulder. But nothing was out of place. Then the sound of a voice reached her from up ahead, along with the staccato *clip clop* of heels. As the sound grew closer, she recognized the voice as Director Drizwold's.

"... apparently we have to drop everything and jump

whenever she says so, and then she changes her mind and the jumping was for nothing." She rounded the corner, and Raven saw her speaking to a mirror. "No, dear," she said after a pause. "I don't mean actual jumping. I mean that I was asked to wait for her, and she was supposed to be here *right now*, but instead—" She stopped at the sight of Raven and lowered her mirror. "Raven, what are you doing here so late?"

"Um, just working on my new design. The one to replace the sprite-wing dress."

"Oh. Yes, I suppose you don't have much time to get a whole new outfit done. But you should be working at home, not here. I don't want students running around the college at all hours of the night."

"Of course. I'm sorry. I'm on my way home now." She slipped past the director and moved quickly along the remaining hallways.

She was almost at the entrance when she heard a familiar voice say her name. "Raven. There you are." Flint strode toward her. "I was just wondering whether I should look for you."

"Sorry, I was cleaning up yesterday's mess." She smiled. "I'm glad it's you. I didn't expect my mother to send ..." She trailed off and looked down at her bag with a frown because somehow, for no reason she could think of, it had begun to grow warmer. She tugged the bag open and looked inside, but the sequined shoe blocked her view of the rest of the bag's contents. She pulled it out—

"Oh, ow!"

She let go as her fingers burned, and the shoe would have

hit the floor, but Flint's hands were suddenly there, scooping the shoe from the air. "Get down!" he yelled as he flung the shoe straight through the open doorway onto the college's front steps.

Light and sound and heat exploded, ripping through the air and throwing Raven backward. A shriek escaped her lips, and she braced herself for the impact of her body slamming against the marble floor. It didn't happen. Magic cushioned her fall, catching her momentarily in its embrace before releasing her. With ears ringing and heart hammering in her chest, she pushed herself up and looked into the smokey orange glow of the flames engulfing the entrance of Delphinium College.

CHAPTER FOUR

"THANK YOU, MISS ROSEWOOD," SAID THE GUARDIAN who'd been questioning Raven for the past ten minutes on the lawn outside Delphinium College's front steps. "We'll be in touch if we require any further information from you."

Raven nodded, wrapping her arms more tightly around her chest. A light touch against her elbow made her flinch and twist around. "Sorry," Flint said. He lowered his arms stiffly to his sides, adopting the kind of stance he always took on when standing guard outside her home. Nothing like the laid-back young man she always hung out with on top of the tower. "Are you ready to go home?"

"Um, yes." Raven took one last look at the cracked, smoking steps and the doorway framed with jagged pieces of glass. She swallowed, thinking once again of how close she'd come to night. If she'd spent just a little longer walking back to ance … If Flint had arrived just a little later … "Thank she said hurriedly, grabbing hold of Flint's hand and zing it. "Thank you so much. If you hadn't thrown the …" She shook her head, not wanting to voice her ughts. "How did you know?"

His eyes flicked momentarily to her hand on his. His noulders relaxed. "I'm familiar with explosive spells. The heat shimmer in the air, the smell." He removed a stylus from an inside pocket of his jacket. "We should get going if you want to arrive home before your parents."

Raven nodded, dread curling in her stomach. "Do they know yet?"

"Your college director is trying to get hold of them right now, so if they don't already know about the explosion, it won't be long before they do."

"They're going to completely overreact about this," Raven said as Flint wrote with his stylus on the statue of Mella Cascata. "Mom will probably insist on driving me to and from Delph in the carriage every day instead of letting me take the faerie paths. Or, even worse, she'll lock me up inside my own home for the rest of my life so that nothing can happen to me."

An opening to the faerie paths appeared on the statue's leg. "Well, if the worst really does happen," Flint said, holding his hand out to her, "I promise to sneak into your luxury cell to keep you company."

She rolled her eyes but smiled anyway as she placed her hand in his. She pictured the entrance hall of her home, and moments later, light materialized up ahead, revealing the vast circular room, the tall vases filled with flowers, and the staircase. As they walked out of the faerie paths, something occurred to Raven. "Do you have access here?" she asked. "I mean, from the paths into this home?"

"No. No one except you and your parents have access via the paths."

"Oh. So you have to wait outside when you get here every day?"

"Not outside the main gate. Those of us who work here have access to the exterior parts of the property. So I usually arrive around the back and the head of security or his second will let me in."

Raven nodded, feeling silly all of a sudden that she didn't know these things. She decided to change the subject. "Are you finished for the night?"

Flint's gaze moved to the clock behind Raven. "Almost. I've got about ten minutes left."

"I suppose I'm keeping you from doing your job then."

His smile fell a little. "Yes, I guess I should return to my post outside, now that you're safely home."

"Seems silly if you've only got ten minutes left of your shift," Raven said, pushing her hands into her jacket pockets. She wasn't being the least bit subtle, but she couldn't help it. Something about almost having a bomb explode in her bag left her feeling like she didn't want to be alone. "I'm surprised you're the one my mother sent," she added before Flint could protest about having to finish his shift. "She already thinks we have an inappropriate relationship because I *smiled* at you. I doubt she'd want to encourage any more interaction between us."

Flint glanced toward the nearest door before straightening slightly and placing both hands neatly behind his back. "She didn't choose me, actually. She sent the butler to see who was on a break at the time, and I happened to be the lucky guy."

Raven laughed. "Lucky, my ass. You almost wound up killed."

"All part of the job," he said, not sounding the least bit concerned for his safety.

Her fingers played with the scrunched up scrap of paper in her pocket. "I wonder if that shoe was even supposed to be a bomb, or if it was simply an accident. The wrong combination of spells mixed together by a fashion student trying to create something spectacular. I mean, why would someone *want* to blow up part of the college?"

Flint shook his head. "I don't know. I asked the guardians who questioned us if they had any idea what was going on, but they wouldn't say."

"I suppose it isn't right for them to speculate." Raven dropped her hands to her sides and looked around. "Anyway, I expect my parents will arrive at any moment, shrieking about the lack of security at Delph. I doubt seeing the two of us casually chatting in the foyer will help the situation, so I should probably let you go."

Flint smiled. "Good night, Raven."

She watched him walk away before looking up at the clock. Almost ten. She headed for the stairs. As she climbed toward the upper level of the house, she removed the scrap of paper from her pocket and flattened it.

until after eight. Won't be interrupted then.

The paper was torn at one end, and clearly showed only half a message. Raven was hoping for something more interesting—a secret declaration of love from one student to another, perhaps—but this could mean any number of boring things. She lowered the note as she entered her bedroom—

—and found a woman standing there.

For a moment, Raven was too startled to say anything. When she found her voice, she stuttered, "H-How did you get in here?"

"That doesn't matter," the woman said. "Unfortunately, you were in the wrong place at the wrong time tonight. You survived the explosion, and now you know too much."

"But—what? I don't know anything."

"I saw you take that bit of paper from the runway, and I saw you examining it now. If I let you take it to the Guild, they'll find out who's behind this."

"But I wasn't planning to take anything to the Guild. Wait, behind what? What's going on?"

The woman raised her hands, magic crackling at her fingertips.

"Wait, wait. You can take the note," Raven said hastily. "Then I have no way of knowing who's—"

A gust of wind swept the paper from her fingers and sent it spinning and twisting toward the woman. She snapped her fingers. The paper caught fire and burned away within seconds.

"So—so now I have no way of knowing who's involved," Raven said. "And you don't need to hurt me."

The woman gave her a self-pitying look. "But you've seen *me*. Which means you know far too much for me to let you get away."

Sparks shot through the air toward Raven. She threw herself to the side, collided with the wall, and lunged for the tiny green bubble stuck to the edge of the vanity mirror. But an irresistible force tugged her back.

"HELP!" she screamed before magic slammed her onto the floor. The woman raced toward her. Gasping for air that wouldn't come, Raven swung her arms around, reaching for something, anything. Her hand struck the leg of the vanity stool, and she tossed it with all her might. It tumbled onto the floor in front of the woman, who leaped around it easily. Raven grasped the edge of the vanity and pulled herself up. As the woman reached her, Raven smacked her hand against the bubble.

An alarm shrieked through the air.

"Damn you," the woman growled, tugging Raven back by her hair. A knife swept down, slicing the air and heading straight for Raven's throat—

A rush of wind and sparks threw them both across the room. She landed on the woman, who cursed loudly in her ear. Confused and half-blinded from the sparks, Raven kicked and shoved and scrambled away. Something caught hold of her leg.

"Raven!"

She kicked again, her foot connecting with something soft as she looked up and found Flint dashing across the room toward her. Behind him ran another two guards, their glittering, golden weapons at the ready. Flint grabbed her hand and tugged her free of the woman's grip. They fell together against a box of fabric. "Don't let her get away!" Flint yelled as the woman jumped to her feet. He wrapped an arm around Raven, and when she looked down, she found dark space opening on her bedroom floor beside Flint. He pulled her against him, and they fell into the nothingness of the faerie paths.

CHAPTER
FIVE

THEY LANDED ON A PAISLEY PATTERNED RUG. FLINT GRASPED Raven's shoulders. "Are you okay?"

Breathing heavily, she blinked and swallowed. "I—I think so. That was ... just ... wow, I am so useless at defending myself." She took in another deep breath. "What in all fae is going on? She said someone was behind the explosion, and that paper I picked up would tell the Guild who it was, and that I knew too much because I'd seen her, and—"

"Hey, calm down." Flint squeezed her shoulders. "Those guardians will take her in. They'll question her, and they'll probably question you again, and they'll sort this whole thing out."

She nodded and finally took a proper look at her surroundings. "Where are we?"

Flint's eyes darted around the small living room they'd landed in. He appeared as surprised as she was, despite the fact that he'd been the one directing the faerie paths. "Oh. I'm sorry. This must have been my first thought." His gaze returned to her. "I'll take you to the Guild instead. It's more appropriate for you to wait there while—"

"Is this your home?" Raven asked, taking another look around the room. It was more plainly decorated than any of the rooms in her parents' home, but the upholstery was good quality, and some thought had definitely gone into the color palette.

"Uh …" Flint hesitated, which was odd, since it wasn't a difficult question. "Yes," he finally said.

"Can we wait here instead?"

"Raven," he said slowly, "the Guild is where I'm expected to take you if something like this happens."

Looking again at her surroundings, and overlaying them with an image of one of her parents' lavish lounges, Flint's unease suddenly made sense. "I'm sorry." She stood. "You're uncomfortable with me being in your home. It's … it's fine. We can go to the Guild."

His eyes widened. "No—I mean—that isn't what I mean. Of course I don't mind you being in my home." His laugh came out sounding far from natural. "This is just … extremely unprofessional of me. My priority is your safety, and my first thought should have been the Guild, not here."

She smiled. "Your home must be safe if it was your first thought."

Flint relaxed a little. "It is. We have all the regular protective spells on the exterior of the tree. But I should still take you to the Guild. I … well, I don't want your parents dismissing me at the end of all this."

"Of course. I understand."

"Flint, what's going—Oh, hello."

Raven turned at the sound of a woman's voice. She stood at the bottom of the stairs with a girl probably a few years younger than Raven just behind her. Their sleepy eyes and messy hair—blonde, but with the same shade of green that streaked through Flint's dark hair—suggested they'd both been in bed before Flint and Raven arrived here. "Hi," Raven said uncertainly, wishing she could remember Flint's surname so she could address his mother properly.

The woman tied the belt of her gown and patted her hair. "Flint, is everything okay?"

"Yes, sorry, I'm just taking Raven to the Guild. There was a—disturbance. At her house."

A frown briefly pulled at his mother's features, but it was gone a moment later. "Okay."

"I'm so sorry we woke you," Raven said. "We'll be on our way now. And Flint's shift is over, so I'm sure he'll be back home soon."

The girl moved forward so that she stood on the same step as her mother. "You're Raven Rosewood?" she asked. "From the house Flint works at?"

Raven opened her mouth to respond, but Flint's mother got there first. "Go back to bed, Tora," she said quietly. "You shouldn't be up this late on a school night."

Tora grinned at her brother before swinging around and hurrying up the stairs.

"I'm so sorry," Raven repeated. "We're leaving right now. I hope you, um, don't have too much trouble getting back to sleep." She hastily patted her jacket, feeling for a stylus, but remembered she didn't have one on her. She looked at Flint.

"Right. Yes. Uh, see you in the morning, Mom."

He opened a faerie paths doorway on the wall, grabbed Raven's hand, and the two of them hurried into the darkness. They walked out on the other side into a tangled forest. Flint took a step forward and raised his hand to write against the nearest tree. At first Raven assumed he was opening another doorway to the paths, but then she noticed the words weren't the same. A moment later, the tree began to change. Its leaves were sucked into the branches, and the branches merged with the trunk. As the trunk widened, glass doors materialized at its center. Stairs pushed outward from the roots. When everything stopped moving, a golden, brightly lit entrance stood before them.

"Come on," Flint said, leading her up the stairs. "Sorry for the whole magical display, but for visitors who have nothing to do with the Guild, this is the only way in." At the top of the stairs, where a guard stood waiting, Flint held up one hand. The guard used her stylus to scan the dark swirling patterns on Flint's wrist. Then he had to explain why Raven was there, fill in a scroll the woman seemed to produce from nowhere, and place a narrow leather band around Raven's wrist. "It will be removed on your way out," the guard told Raven as she watched a symbol glow briefly on the band before vanishing.

"If you don't work here," Raven whispered to Flint as they walked inside, "why do you still have guardian markings on your wrists?"

Numerous doors led off the foyer of the Guild, and Flint moved toward one on the right. "As long as I'm still working as a guardian, I'll always have the markings. That doesn't change just because I'm not working at a particular Guild." He took her along a corridor and into a comfortable waiting area with plenty of seats scattered around and a desk on one side. Flint nodded at the man behind the desk. "We can sit here until your parents arrive," he said to Raven.

She chose a couch and sat down. While she didn't want to be left alone in this unfamiliar place, she didn't want to keep Flint here when his shift was finished. "You don't have to wait with me," she told him. "I know your duty's over for the night."

"Raven, you're a friend." He sat beside her. "I don't mind waiting with you."

She smiled. It was probably selfish of her, but she was happy to have him stay. She leaned back and pushed her hands through her hair. "I keep thinking of all the things I could have done to better defend myself against that woman. Any of the small things you've taught me over the past few months. But no, I had to throw a stool at her with my bare hands, for goodness sake. What happened to throwing it with magic? What happened to releasing *any* form of magic? That would have been better than scrambling around like a helpless human. Not," she added quickly at the sight of Flint's raised eyebrows, "that I have anything against humans. They could probably have done better than me tonight because they don't have magic, so they're prepared in different ways."

"Trust me," Flint said, "most of them are not prepared for an assault of any kind, let alone a magical one."

Raven sighed. "Look, this isn't about humans. This is about my embarrassing lack of self-defense skills."

"Have you seen me try to cast an article of clothing before?"

"Well, no." She tilted her head to the side and gave Flint a sly grin. "I doubt you could even cast a button back on."

"Exactly. We all have different skills. At least you have *some* skills in the self-defense department, based on the few things I've taught you."

"I still feel pretty useless right now."

He stuck his hand out, palm up. "Give me a button. I'll soon make you feel less useless."

She chuckled. "If I had one, I'd give it to you, just so we'd have something amusing to pass the time with. Sadly, I don't." She looked around the room once more, then stood up to examine some of the paintings on the walls. When she reached a mirror, she was startled by her appearance. Her floral jacket was smudged with dark smoke and torn across the left sleeve, and the white shirt beneath it was just as dirty. And despite the fact that she'd been thrown across both the college foyer and her bedroom, she could still see at least one feather in her hair. "Flint!" she scolded. "Why didn't you tell me I look so terrible?"

"Hmm?" He looked up from his amber.

"I can't believe your mother saw me looking such a mess. What must she think of me?"

Flint laughed. "I can tell you right now that my mother was far more concerned about appearing in front of *you* in her dressing gown than about anything that might have been wrong with your outfit."

"That can't be true. Her dressing gown was lovely."

"I'll be sure to tell her you think so." He checked his amber again and added, "It's odd that we haven't heard from your parents yet. I thought they'd be here by now."

"I guess." Raven lowered herself back onto the couch. "It isn't hugely surprising, though. Sometimes, if it's a good party, they don't notice that they're missing messages or mirror calls. After Mom sent you to fetch me, she probably assumed her motherly duty was done for the night."

"I'm sorry, Raven. That isn't …" He frowned at his amber again.

"What?" Raven asked.

"Uh …" He paused, reading through the tiny, glowing script that appeared on his amber. "That woman who was in your room. She put up a fight and … well, she's dead."

"Oh. Oh my goodness." Raven's hand rose to cover her mouth for a moment. "But … it's supposed to be quite tough to kill a faerie."

"Yes," Flint said quietly.

"It must have been quite a fight." She leaned forward on her elbows, shaking her head. "And the thing is, it hadn't even occurred to me to take that piece of paper to the Guild. I didn't think it was related to the explosion. I probably would have thrown it away. This woman got herself killed for nothing."

"So senseless," Flint murmured.

They continued to chat quietly while they waited, and it was almost midnight by the time Raven's parents showed up. Zalea ran toward her daughter, the glittering tassels of her dress flapping around her knees. "Oh, what a relief," she said, wrapping Raven tightly in a hug. "You see?" she said when she stepped back. "I told you it was dangerous to stay late at college."

"Mom." Raven said patiently. "This is the first time something like this has ever happened at Delph. It was just an unfortunate coincidence that I happened to be on the premises at the same time. I think we should be more concerned about the fact that someone got into my bedroom."

"That is definitely of great concern," her father Kenrick said. "I'd like to know how that happened."

"Apparently no one at the front gate saw anything unusual, sir," Flint said, standing straight and stiff and staring over her father's shoulder while he spoke. "The guards patrolling the walls saw nothing either. It's possible that Raven and I were followed through the faerie paths."

Zalea clicked her tongue and rolled her eyes. "Impossible," she muttered.

Raven watched Flint open his mouth, then shut it again, clearly deciding it was best not to argue with her mother.

"Thank you for waiting with Raven," Kenrick said to Flint. "You're dismissed now."

Raven cringed at her father's words, spoken to Flint as if he were a servant. "Good night," she murmured as he left.

"I'll speak to our head of security the moment we get

home," Kenrick said to Zalea. "If the protective spells around the house aren't the absolute latest, he's fired."

"And if they are, he needs to explain how this happened," Zalea added, "and then add more spells. Another few layers of protection should stop this from happening again."

"Great," Raven said to her parents. "So everything's okay then?"

Zalea crossed her arms and faced Raven. "Extra protective spells aren't enough. When it comes to my daughter, I want every security measure we can afford."

"Agreed," Kenrick said.

Raven raised both eyebrows, not liking the sound of where this was going. "What exactly does that mean?"

Zalea hesitated a moment too long before speaking. "It means you need a bodyguard."

Raven's mouth dropped open. "I do *not* need a bodyguard."

"I won't let you leave the house without one. It's your choice."

"That isn't a choice at all, Mom."

"Well, it's the only choice you're getting. Either allow a trained guardian to accompany you everywhere, or leave Delphinium College and remain at home where I know you're safe."

Raven shook her head slowly. "You wouldn't make me leave Delph without graduating. It would be just as much of an embarrassment to you as to me. You won't be able to brag about me and my bright future to all your friends if I don't finish college and get that internship."

Zalea blinked and looked down. Her voice was uncharacteristically quiet when she spoke. "Perhaps not, but at least my daughter will still be alive."

Raven hadn't meant it earlier when she'd told Flint her mother might lock her up in her own house after this incident, but it seemed she'd been far closer to the truth than she could have imagined. "Fine." She folded her arms over her chest, matching her mother's stance. "Then I get to choose the guard."

Zalea paused, her lips pursing together for a moment. "All right. Who do you want?"

Raven raised her chin just the slightest, daring her mother to contradict her. "Flint."

"Flint?" Zalea gazed blankly at her. "Which one is that?"

Raven's shoulders slumped in disbelief. "The one who saved my life tonight. Twice."

"Oh, the one who was just standing here?" Zalea said with disdain, gold bangles jingling around her arm as she waved to the empty spot Flint had occupied until minutes ago. "But he's the youngest guard we've ever had. Far too inexperienced. What about Rex?" she suggested, referring to the guard who often accompanied Raven's father to evening meetings. "He's been in private security for at least a hundred and fifty years."

"I don't want some old man following me around everywhere, Mom. It's weird. This whole bodyguard idea is weird. At least if it's someone closer to my own age I don't have to feel like a naughty child you're trying to keep an eye on."

Kenrick's brow creased as he stroked his chin in consideration. "How old is … what did you say his name was?"

"Flint."

"He's only twenty-one," Zalea said.

"Twenty-two," Raven corrected.

Zalea narrowed her eyes. "Didn't I speak to you about inappropriate relationships with our employees? Exactly how well do you know this young man?"

"I know that he's been with us for almost a year, which means he's a year older than when you hired him."

"He did come with an excellent letter of recommendation from the Guild," Kenrick said. "I remember that. It's the only reason we consented to employ a guard so young. And he's already proved himself by protecting Raven twice tonight." He let out a long breath and pushed both hands into his pockets. "I think we can probably trust him with Raven's safety."

"*Probably?*" Zalea repeated. "We need more than probably."

"You can trust him, Mom. There's no probably about it. He risked his life for me tonight."

"Fine." Zalea turned to her husband. "Can you make sure this guard—Flint—is informed of his new duty tomorrow?"

"Of course."

"And he's not following me around college," Raven added. "That would be a total embarrassment, and a total waste of his time."

"College is where you were almost hurt. I won't let you walk around there without—"

"The college would never allow it," Raven said, sincerely hoping her words were true. "It would be a complete disruption to our classes to have someone following me everywhere. What if every student wanted a bodyguard? There'd be no space for us all. Besides, I'm sure Delph will increase their security after this incident."

"Raven—"

"Flint can accompany me to and from college. If I go shopping or to Daisy's or to one of your parties or *anywhere* else, he can come with. But I will not be babysat at my school."

A painfully long moment of silence passed before Zalea nodded brusquely. Then she swept past Raven, leaning closer to her husband and muttering, "This stubborn streak of hers comes entirely from you."

CHAPTER SIX

WHISPERS FOLLOWED RAVEN AROUND COLLEGE ON Monday. Fortunately, they were the only thing that followed her. Flint accompanied her through the faerie paths and around to the back entrance of Delphinium—the front entrance was closed off for now—and waited to leave until after she'd entered the building. It felt unnecessary to Raven, but at the same time, she enjoyed Flint's company.

In class, the subject on everyone's lips was the explosion. Lessons had ended for the year, and everyone was supposed to be finishing off their collections for the final show. Instead, they gathered in small groups around each other's desks and discussed their theories about the explosion.

"So guess what I heard," Poe said, leaning against Raven's desk along with Jessima, his closest friend.

"Can I first ask how reliable your source is," Raven said, "before you go spreading around whatever it is that you 'heard'?"

"Hey, this information is legit. I was around the corner when two guardians were speaking to the director this morning. This is proper eavesdropping we're talking about here."

"I'm not sure you should be proud of that," Jessima said.

"Yeah, okay, whatever." Poe waved at her to keep quiet. "I heard the director telling the guardians that Mella Cascata was supposed to meet her here on Friday night. Something about preparations for the final show. So perhaps—" he paused dramatically "—that bomb was meant for the great Madame Cascata."

With a frown, Raven thought back to the mirror conversation she'd overheard the director having on Friday night. She'd spoken about having to wait for someone who didn't show up. A woman who expected everyone to jump whenever she said so. That sounded like it was probably Mella Cascata.

"You think someone wanted to kill Mella Cascata?" Jessima said. "More likely someone wanted to kill the director."

"Or the *director* wanted to kill *Mella*," Poe said.

"But why?" Raven asked. "Why would anyone want to kill either of them?"

In conspiratorial tones, Poe said, "Who knows what drama is going on behind the scenes?"

"Come, come, come, girls and boys," Director Drizwold said, clapping her hands as she walked into the room. "What's going on in here? Why is no one working? Where's your teacher?"

"Girls and boys," Jessima whispered. "Now there's a reason why someone might want to get rid of her. Why does she insist on calling us that?"

"So sorry," Cecilia said, hurrying into the room with a basket of scrolls gliding behind her. "Those guardians wanted to speak with me, and they went on a bit too long. I'll take over from here. Everyone—" she raised her voice "—please return to your own desks. I have the results of your last test here."

Director Drizwold dodged beneath an escaped feather boa sailing across the classroom, glared at the nearest student, and left. Collective relief rippled around the room, and faint chatter started up again as Cecilia handed out the scrolls. Friendly but firm, and a remarkably talented clothes caster, Cecilia was Raven's favorite teacher. The favorite teacher of most students, in fact. Raven knew she wasn't the only one who wished Cecilia took them for more than three lessons a week.

After handing out the tests, Cecilia did the rounds. She assisted students with complex spells, helped with last-minute ideas, or gave feedback on work already done. Raven was desperate to hear Cecilia's thoughts on her new snake dress idea, but the bell that signaled the end of classes for the day tinkled before Cecilia reached her row.

"If I haven't seen you yet," Cecilia called out as students began packing up, "and you'd like my feedback, please wait behind."

Raven was one of four who remained in the classroom. While she waited for her turn, she went through her spell books and wrote down the incantations she'd need to incorporate in order for the metal snake to slither in a winding pattern up her model's back. She hadn't fully decided what to do with the rest of the dress, but she searched for spells that made use of lavagem light, mainly because most other students wouldn't use those spells.

When Cecilia had finished speaking to the other three students, she stood in front of Raven's desk with her lips turned down. "I'm so sorry your demo went wrong yesterday. That dress would have made a spectacular final piece for your collection. I just assumed it would go through."

"Me too," Raven said. "I'm so disappointed. I love that dress more than anything else I've made this year."

Cecilia leaned her hip against the desk. "Honestly, I think you could still make it work with just a few minor adjustments, but if the director decided not to approve it, then that's it. Best to move on with something else."

"I know. So I've got this snake idea now. A snake slithering across a forest floor of leaves." Raven turned her notebook around to face Cecilia. "I'm going to do the snake like this on the back, winding back and forth as it slithers upward. And then perhaps cover the entirety of the rest of the dress in leaves. Like that autumn dress I did once, remember? But I'll have the leaves coming up over one shoulder, and have the dress reach the floor, and I won't use an autumn palette, of course. I'll use these colors here—" she grabbed a few swatches from her desk and pulled them closer "—to fit in with the rest of my collection."

Cecilia smiled and nodded slowly. "I have to admit, I was a little worried when I heard Director Drizwold hadn't approved

the sprite-wing dress, but this could be just as magnificent."
She chuckled. "You never cease to amaze me, Raven. You
could be the next Mella Cascata, you know. You *should* be the
next Mella Cascata, whether you win that internship or not."

Raven flushed with pleasure at the compliment. "Thank
you." Her voice lowered to a whisper as she added, "But you
probably shouldn't let any of her many worshippers hear that
you're hoping someone will replace her. Besides, *you're* more
likely to be the next Mella Cascata. You know far more about
this industry than I do, and I would kill to have your kind of
skill with clothes casting spells. *And* you kinda look like her.
You're the perfect package."

Surprise crossed Cecilia's face. "You think I look like her?"

"Well, just a little bit," Raven corrected as she realized
Cecilia might not consider that a compliment. "Why did you
choose teaching anyway? I'm sure you could have made it on
your own, or at one of the big houses."

A sad smile crossed Cecilia's face before she looked down
and began neatening the contents of Raven's desk, pushing
aside and folding up the fabric she wouldn't be using and
moving all the jars of embellishments into neat rows. "I didn't
have the right opportunities at the right time, and my family
suggested the teaching route would be appropriate for me. I've
enjoyed it. Enjoyed discovering new talent like yours. Anyway—" she tucked her hands behind her back "—here's my
feedback on the snake idea."

Raven grabbed her sketch and got ready to add notes to it.
Cecilia didn't have too many things to say, so she was done in a
few minutes. "Thanks," Raven said as she packed her things

away into her bag, a deep green one that matched the green in the checkered pattern of her pants. "I'll get to work on making this one as soon as possible."

"Yes, you haven't got much time left. Try not to get too distracted by anything else this week."

"Hmm. Easier said than done when your parents expect you to attend most of the events they attend." She pulled her bag onto her shoulder. "Will you be at the Harlington Home fundraiser tonight? I heard you mention it to someone earlier."

"Oh, no, no." Cecilia shook her head. "I'd love to, but my, uh, *husband* … doesn't care for such things." The way she ground out the word 'husband' was odd, but Raven wasn't about to ask Cecilia if there were issues going on in her marriage. That definitely wouldn't be appropriate. "Well, I need to get going," she added, picking up the amber she'd left on Raven's desk.

"Oh, me too." It had been a while since classes ended, and Raven suddenly remembered that Flint would be waiting for her outside. Along with feeling bad knowing how long he must have been standing out there, she felt a spark of anticipation. It was fun getting to interact with him more than just once a week on a Thursday night. She'd never admit it to her mother, but this bodyguard idea might actually be a good one.

CHAPTER SEVEN

"SO THERE WAS A DEAD BODY RIGHT HERE IN YOUR bedroom?" Daisy wrapped her satin robe tightly around herself, wide eyes traveling the room, as if the ghost of the intruder woman might be hiding somewhere watching her.

"I'd prefer it if you didn't remind me of that," Raven said. She hadn't been allowed into her room when she and her parents had returned late last night. It was considered a crime scene, apparently. Her mother had made a gigantic fuss, insisted the guardians work through the night gathering whatever evidence they needed, then kicked them out this morning. By the time Raven left for college, the maids had already begun cleaning, and when she returned late this afternoon, she'd found her bedroom in perfect order. No trace of the previous night's fight was anywhere to be seen. Still, as Daisy pointed out, it was hard not to think about the fact that someone had died in here. Raven had a feeling it wouldn't be so easy to fall asleep tonight.

Pushing the thought of dead bodies aside, she walked into her closet and fetched the blue dress for Daisy and the black lace one she'd chosen for herself. A mermaid style, with long sleeves and a low back, it was elegant, understated, and far less fun than anything she designed at college. A public evening event, her mother had told her years ago, was not an appropriate occasion for frivolous outfits. Raven was expected to be refined, poised—boring. Good thing she'd had plenty of practice at that over the years.

"I think it's a little tight on me," Daisy said. Raven turned to find Daisy clutching the dress around her upper body and trying to do the back up. She pulled her shoulders up and sucked her stomach in. "My mom must have been right when she said I was getting fat."

"Your mom needs a slap if she's saying things like that to you."

Daisy started laughing. "I'd love to see that. You slapping my mom."

"I'm sorry, I know it's rude of me, but seriously?" Raven crossed the room and picked up her stylus from her desk. "She said you're getting fat? What a load of goblin crap. You're a slightly different shape than I am, that's all. And this is a fitted dress, so the shape is important. Here, I'll make the adjustments while it's on you. It'll be quick." She ran her stylus across the fabric here and there, expanding some parts and shrinking others. "There." She stepped back when she was done. "More comfortable?"

"Well, I can breathe, so that's an improvement."

"That's a bonus, as they like to say at Delph," Raven said with a laugh.

After doing each other's hair—fingers weaving quick enchantments to produce elegant updos—they added the finishing jewelry and makeup touches to their outfits. Lastly, Raven stepped into her latest high-heeled creation.

"Wow, those are amazing," Daisy said as she pulled her own shoes on.

"Aren't they just?" Pride swelled in Raven's chest as she looked down at her jewel-encrusted shoes. She'd spent an entire weekend on them recently, arranging the different colored precious stones into various shapes, and they'd turned out even better than she'd imagined. "I'm probably pushing the limits of what my mother considers acceptable evening footwear—too much twinkling color—but I think people will love them."

Daisy nodded. "I think you're right."

"Ready to go?"

"Almost." Daisy turned and examined her appearance in the floor-length mirror standing in one corner. "I need a touch more makeup, perhaps."

As Daisy played with makeup spells, Raven walked to her door. She opened it, taking in a quick breath when she saw a figure standing several feet away. She relaxed as she recognized Flint. "Good evening, Miss Rosewood," he said, which must mean other members of her household were close enough to overhear him. His eyes skimmed down her dress before looking quickly—politely—away. A hint of a smile grew on his lips, though, which in turn made Raven smile. She liked it when people admired her creations.

"Good evening, Flint," she said in equally formal tones before lowering her voice and adding, "Sorry about the gasp thing. I still need to get used to opening my door and finding someone waiting for me." And she'd have to get used to seeing him dressed in something other than the usual uniform her parents' guards wore. As her personal protector, he was supposed to blend in with the crowd, not stand out as a target for someone to aim at before taking Raven out. Or something like that. She hadn't listened to everything her father rambled on about this morning.

"No, I apologize," Flint said, his eyes still averted. "I didn't mean to startle you. In fact, I think that's the opposite of what a personal bodyguard is supposed to do."

"I'm sorry about all this. It must really suck for you. Having to attend boring parties you don't care about. It's more like a punishment than a promotion." She laughed and added, "I probably should have asked for the guard I like least instead of asking for you."

His smile stretched a little wider. "Nothing to be sorry about. I can assure you I don't see this as a punishment."

"I'm glad." Raven looked over her shoulder. "Daisy, come on. What's taking so long?"

"Stupid lipstick spell went wrong," Daisy called back to her.

Raven shook her head and returned her gaze to Flint. "You look nice in formal wear." His suit jacket, slightly longer than an everyday jacket, with buttons all the way up to the high-necked collar, hinted at a more traditional design Raven didn't see too often these days. It was a classic look that Flint pulled off remarkably well.

His gaze turned back to her for the first time since she'd opened the door. "You also look, um ... very nice."

"Okay, okay, I'm ready." Daisy rushed through the doorway and almost ran into Raven. "Oh, hi," she said to Flint before turning back to Raven. "Um, are we going now?"

"Yes." Raven slipped her arm through her friend's and headed for the stairs, looking over the railing down to the entrance hall to see if her parents were ready yet.

"He really is following you everywhere," Daisy whispered with a giggle.

"Shh." Raven threw a glance over her shoulder, but Flint was looking down at the entrance hall as he walked several feet behind them. "Not everywhere. And it's not as though I mind. It's like having a friend travel around with me."

"A friend who has to pretend he isn't your friend whenever your parents happen to be nearby."

"Yes, well, it's just easier that way."

In the carriage, Raven and Daisy sat on one side with Flint, while Zalea and Kenrick sat opposite them. Kenrick issued instructions to Flint from the moment the carriage took off, which caused Raven to feel more and more uncomfortable. "Maintain a respectable distance, but make sure to keep Raven in sight at all times. Try to remain inconspicuous. Don't dance with anyone. And don't speak to people. You're not there to be distracted."

"Dad," Raven interrupted as her discomfort level reached new heights. "I'm sure Flint knows all of this already."

Her father managed to remain quiet the rest of the way there, and other than the occasional whisper between Raven and Daisy, the carriage's occupants sat in uncomfortable silence. Fortunately, the journey wasn't long, and the carriage soon pulled up outside Mount Thistlewood Country Club. This evening's fundraiser was being held in support of Harlington Home for Orphaned Fae, a home started decades ago by one of Zalea's friends. The fundraiser was an annual event, and Raven and her parents always attended.

The high-ceilinged room was already packed when they arrived, filled with glamorous, wealthy and influential fae. Dressed in nothing but the latest and best, they moved between long tables piled high with delicacies, gossiping, laughing, and bidding on the artwork displayed around the edge of the room.

For the first time, Raven wondered how all this obscene extravagance appeared to someone like Flint. Someone who lived in an ordinary home hidden by a glamour. Someone who wasn't wearing a designer suit and who didn't play around with disgustingly large amounts of money on a regular basis. She looked at every gleaming surface, every gold-plated piece of cutlery, and every rare item of food through his eyes, knowing that all the money spent on this event could have gone toward the worthy cause everyone here claimed to support instead of enabling a bunch of rich fae to party it up for the night. In fact, if she'd been Flint, she might have stormed out at the sight of all this wasted wealth. But Flint maintained his composure perfectly, and if there was anything about this event that bothered him, he didn't show it.

It bothered Raven, though, and not for the first time. And it pricked at her conscience that she was once again part of the lavish, high-society scenery instead of ... Instead of what? she wondered. Instead of refusing to come? Instead of telling the organizers of these events that they should give their money straight to the cause they were fundraising for? But she knew it didn't work that way. Most of the guests here wouldn't bother supporting anything if there wasn't a party involved. This would probably be an extremely worthwhile event in the end, despite the unnecessary display of opulence. Still, Raven felt more uncomfortable than she'd ever felt at a party before.

"Oh, look over there," Daisy said, motioning to the left with a nod of her head. "Isn't that what's-his-name? Lilyanna's cousin? He's got real nerve attending another public event after the way he behaved at your eighteenth a few weeks ago. I'm surprised his parents let him out of the house."

Raven shrugged. "Maybe it wasn't his fault he ate all those moonflower petals. I mean, maybe he didn't know the effect they would have."

"Hah," Daisy snorted. "I'll bet he knew exactly what he was doing."

"Well, let's hope he behaves himself tonight," Raven said, surveying the nearest table of food. She didn't particularly feel like eating anything, but she didn't feel like engaging in conversation with anyone either. She looked over her shoulder, her eyes searching the crowd until they landed on Flint. He was hovering near the door they'd come in through.

"Oh no," Daisy whispered. "There he is."

Raven knew without having to ask—without having to turn

back and look, though that's exactly what she did—who Daisy was referring to. "Orson," she muttered. "Now there's someone who shouldn't have been let out of the house."

"I'm, uh …" Daisy cleared her throat. "I'm going to go say hi to my sister. I just noticed her over there."

"Daisy," Raven said, but Daisy was already walking away, weaving through the crowd. She hoped Daisy really had just noticed her sister, and that she wasn't acting strangely all of a sudden because of Orson.

Since she'd taken the time to dress up for this event, she may as well show off her latest creation. She picked up a glass of something bubbly, then walked around the room, making sure her shoes were visible beneath the swishing edge of her black dress. She politely greeted anyone who looked her way, and thanked those who commented on her shoes. A few of her mother's friends inquired about her collection for the final show, and two girls from Delphinium College stopped her to rehash every detail of Friday night's explosion.

"Oh, Raven, there you are." Zalea grabbed Raven's arm just as she was attempting to extricate herself from the never-ending discussion with the two Delph girls. "Look who it is. Orson was just telling me how he thought you were the prettiest girl in the room at the Lavisons' union ceremony last year. You didn't tell me the two of you were well acquainted already."

"Not that well acquainted," Raven corrected, meeting Orson's eyes—a blue so dark it was almost black—with a level gaze. She'd once been captivated by those alluring eyes. A silly girl reduced to giggles and blushing. She knew better now.

"Lovely Raven," Orson said, his hand rising to briefly caress her cheek. Raven considered ripping that hand right off his arm, but remembered her instructions to Daisy about not making a scene. "If you don't feel we know each other well enough," he purred, "we'll have to change that."

Raven looked to see how her mother would react to that one, but Zalea seemed charmed. Seriously? Hadn't she noticed what a slimy character Orson had turned out to be?

"Still playing with pretty dresses, I see," Orson said. His eyes lingered on Raven's form, and for some reason her mind flashed back to that moment when Flint had looked at her earlier. It struck her how entirely different that moment had been from this one. Orson's suggestive gaze made her skin crawl, while Flint's quickly averted eyes and stumbling, awkward compliment of her dress had left her smiling.

"Yes, and she's become quite good at dress casting," Zalea answered for her with a tinkling, high-pitched laugh that grated at Raven's nerves. "We expect her to win the internship at the House of Cascata. I'm sure fine fae all over the world will be wearing Raven creations one day."

"I'm sure they will," Orson said, and as her mother turned away to greet someone else, he added in a low tone, "and tearing them off one another in the heat of passion."

With a sweet smile, Raven said, "You're disgusting."

Still watching her with those hypnotizing eyes, he chuckled. "You know you love it."

"I'd love nothing more right now than to get away from you."

"Well, I'll let you go soon enough. But first, who's the pup who followed you in here?"

"You'll need to be more specific if you'd like me to have even the vaguest idea what you're talking about."

"Is he the secret bodyguard all your Delph classmates have been whispering about since the explosion that almost blew your pretty head off? If so, he isn't doing a very good job at blending in."

Raven followed Orson's gaze to where Flint was standing near a sculpture, hands clasped behind his back, looking awkward. He met Raven's eyes briefly before looking away. "He's a friend," Raven said. "I don't need a bodyguard, Orson. I can take care of myself." And how she wished that were true right now.

"For a friend, he isn't being particularly friendly. And what is he wearing? An antique suit?"

"You wouldn't know classic fashion if it wrapped itself around your neck and started strangling you."

Orson laughed. "Classic. That's one way of putting it."

"That's the professionals' way of putting it," Raven snapped, noticing a few unintentional sparks of angry magic escaping her tongue. "It isn't his fault you can't tell the difference between a well-made suit and the piece of garbage you're wearing. Probably put together by a bunch of gob—"

"Opaline! Woody! Where have you two been hiding?" Orson waved across the crowd at two of his friends. "You'll have to excuse me, Raven darling," Orson said to her. "I have better company to attend to. Oh, and there's Daisy." He gave Raven a wicked grin. "She and I certainly have some catching up to do, preferably in a private room upstairs if all our previous interactions are anything to go by."

Raven's hand clenched around her glass. She considered throwing its contents in Orson's face, but he was already moving swiftly away. Forcing herself to take a deep breath and remember that Orson only said these kinds of things to get her worked up, she looked around for a distraction—and saw Daisy. Daisy stood on the far side of the room with her older sister and a few other friends, but her eyes were on Raven. She looked away quickly, her frown vanishing as she forced a not-so-natural smile onto her face.

Stupid Orson, Raven thought. Messing with her friendship with Daisy all over again. She set her drink down on a passing tray and began moving through the crowd toward her friend, but Daisy looped her arm through her sister's and headed into the next room where more auction items lined the walls.

Raven slowed to a halt. The desire to abandon this party and hide herself amongst a mound of fabric and idea-filled notebooks overwhelmed her. But she couldn't leave. It would upset her mother, and that might end with Raven locked inside her own house after all. Her gaze landed on Flint, still looking far too awkward. He caught her eye and smiled. Spirits lifting, Raven pushed through the crowd toward him. "Do you know how to dance?" she asked when she reached his side.

His eyebrows jumped the tiniest bit. "Dance? I think the last time I danced—this kind of dancing—was at my graduation ball. But I can probably remember most of the steps."

"Do you want to dance with me?"

"Oh." His surprise was followed by a wide grin. "I do actually, but I think 'don't dance with anyone' was on the long list of instructions your father gave me in the carriage."

"True, but one of the other instructions was to remain inconspicuous. And I'm sorry—" she stepped a little closer, trying to keep the teasing tone from her voice "—but you haven't exactly succeeded at that so far."

"I was told not to be distracted by speaking to anyone, so I can't help but look a little bit like an idiot just standing here."

"Oh, I didn't say you were conspicuous because you look like an idiot. Quite the opposite. It's conspicuous for a man who looks so dashing to be standing all on his own. I'm surprised half the ladies in this room haven't come flocking to introduce themselves to you." Goodness, was she flirting? She almost giggled as she realized she was. "Anyway," she hurried on as her skin heated, "I'm glad they didn't because that would have made your job more difficult. But since I'm the one you're supposed to be watching, it should be fine for you to dance with me."

Flint looked down, his smile fading just a little. "I'd rather not embarrass you or your parents."

"Oh." Raven nodded, annoyed that she felt so disappointed.

"But," he added quickly, "you could explain to me what all this food is. I don't recognize half of it, and I'm not sure I should be eating things I can't name."

Raven laughed. "To be honest, I can't name half these food items either. I've probably tasted everything at some point or another, because clearly I don't have the same concerns you have about eating food I don't recognize, but that doesn't mean I know what any of it is."

"Well, if you've survived it all, it can't be that bad."

"Oh, no, some of it's horrible. Those little balls over there with the tiny black spikes are disgusting." She pointed to a dish on the table behind Flint, then leaned closer and whispered, "They look like they would poke the inside of your mouth, but they're actually slimy and squishy and taste like feet."

Flint whispered back, "Should I ask how you know what feet taste like?"

She laughed. "Probably not."

They passed the remainder of the evening this way, discussing the food, the people, the outfits, and the artworks. Zalea caught Raven's eye at one point, gave a brief but unhappy shake of her head and a pointed glare in Flint's direction. Her message was clear, but Raven chose to ignore it. If her parents insisted on this bodyguard idea, then she would spend as much time with that bodyguard as she wanted.

CHAPTER EIGHT

"HAVE YOU SEEN THE NEW ENTRANCE?" POE ASKED RAVEN the following morning as he leaned against her desk. Apparently he didn't have much of his own work to get on with. "And the two guardians stationed out there?"

"Yes. How do you think I got inside the building this morning?"

"Well I don't know," he said defensively. "Maybe you used the back entrance."

Raven sighed. "Sorry. I'm know I'm being snappish. I just have so much to get done in the next few days." She'd almost finished fashioning the metal snake for the back of her dress. That was the easy part, though. The spells she'd need to apply to it would take more time. She paged through her notes, looking for the enchantments she'd planned to add to the snake eyes.

"Hey, is Cecilia taking us today?" Poe asked. "That wasn't on the class schedule."

Raven looked up as Cecilia hurried in and headed straight for her desk, looking slightly flustered. "Hey there, guys," she said to them.

"Cecilia, you're the best." Poe gave her a sideways hug. "Have you come to rescue us from Mundy? He isn't nearly as good as you are at all this stuff."

"Shh, don't say things like that," Cecilia chided while clearly trying to keep her smile hidden. "Mundy is a very capable teacher. And perhaps you'd be better at this 'stuff,' Poe, if you were working on it at your own desk instead of lounging around distracting Raven."

Raven laughed, while Poe pretended to be deeply wounded. "Fine," he grumbled as he walked away. "You're probably right."

"Sorry I can't stay long," Cecilia said to Raven. "I just wanted to tell you something quickly. I was thinking that perhaps you should bring the sprite-wing dress back to college. I know you can't use it for the final show, but if we fix it up and make sure it's working properly, I have a few events in mind that it might be perfect for."

"Really?" Raven sat forward. "That would be wonderful."

"Great. I'll tell you more about it another day when I'm in less of a rush."

"Thanks, Cecilia," Raven called after her as she hastened from the room. Bella, sitting at her desk near the front, looked over her shoulder and caught Raven's eye. Her dirty look told Raven exactly what she was thinking: *the favored Raven Rosewood.* Raven ignored Bella and turned back to her work, trying not to let the other girl's reaction bother her.

After the final tinkling of the bell at the end of the day, Raven bundled up all the pieces of her dress into her bag and left the classroom quickly. She strode along the hallways to the other side of the college where the design students spent most of their time. Daisy hadn't spoken to her since they'd spotted Orson at the fundraiser last night. She'd left with her sister after the auction winners were announced and hadn't replied to the messages Raven sent her this morning.

"Hey, Daisy, wait," Raven shouted as she spotted her friend coming out of one of the studios.

Daisy looked back with a startled expression. Raven half expected her to bolt, but she stayed where she was, giving Raven a small wave and a smile.

"Are you upset with me?" Raven asked when she reached her friend.

"What? No, of course not."

"You didn't look very happy last night after I was forced into conversation with Orson."

"I wasn't upset with you. Seeing *him* upset me." She folded her arms over her chest. "It shouldn't, because I'm not supposed to care about him at all, but he just makes me so *angry.*"

"Yeah. Me too." Raven played with the strap of her bag. "So why did you avoid me all of last night and ignore my messages this morning if he's the one you're upset with?"

Daisy opened her mouth, probably to deny she'd been ignoring anything, then sighed. Her shoulders slumped. "Look, it's just weird. It's the first time we've seen him since, you know … everything blew up with us."

"But I thought you and I were past all that. *He* was the one at fault."

"I know. I'm … I'm sorry." Abruptly, Daisy wrapped her arms around Raven. "Let's not be awkward, okay?"

Raven hugged her back. "Agreed. Let's not be awkward."

They walked together to the brand new college entrance. Raven could sense a kind of prickle upon her skin as she passed through the doorway, a hint of the additional magic that had been added to the college in the past few days. She wasn't sure exactly what it was supposed to prevent or detect, or how it worked, but she sincerely hoped it would prevent scenarios like the one she'd witnessed on Friday night.

She and Daisy walked onto the steps—and there was Orson Willowstack, lounging against one of the pillars and writing on his amber. He looked up, a smug grin appearing on his face at the sight of them. He slipped the amber and his stylus into an inner pocket of his jacket.

"What are you doing here?" Raven asked as Daisy tensed beside her.

"Waiting for someone else, actually, but it's always a lovely surprise to see two of my favorite ladies together."

"Hah." Raven let out a very unladylike snort. "You are so full of—"

"Which unlucky girl has caught your attention this time?" Daisy asked.

Orson's expression grew downcast. "Daisy, I find that very hurtful. I thought we had something special."

The sound that escaped Daisy's throat was almost a growl. "I'll give you something to hurt about." She lunged forward, her hands rising to his neck, but Raven caught her and pulled her back.

Orson chuckled. "Thank you, Raven, for looking out for—"

"Shut up," Raven snapped.

"Raven?"

Relief cooled the heat coursing through her body at the sound of Flint's voice. Looking down, she found him at the bottom of the steps. She would have smiled if not for the expression of concern on his face.

"Ah, look at that," Orson said. "It's your babysitter, Raven. Here to pick you up after school."

Raven's anger returned in an instant, rippling across her body in waves of hot and cold and escaping her right hand in an uncontrolled sizzle of magic. Her attention snapped back to Orson. But of the many insults flying through her mind, not one managed to make its way to her tongue before Flint reached her side.

"Everything okay here?" he asked. Raven was pleased to note how much smaller and weedier Orson looked next to her muscular, Guild-trained 'babysitter.'

"Of course," Orson said as he pulled himself up to his full and unimpressive height. "We're having a marvelous time. Well," he added with a roll of his eyes, "we were until Raven's chaperone showed up." He leaned closer and said in a mock whisper, "You do know you're ruining all her fun, right? She hates that you're following her everywhere. Why don't you do us all a favor and get lost? I'm sure Raven won't tell her parents."

Raven was so appalled at Orson's blatant lies that nothing but a strangled stutter managed to make its way out of her mouth. Flint, on the other hand, remained composed. He folded his arms across his chest and said, "Sounds like a good idea. I'm not quite sure how to *get lost*, though. Perhaps you'd like to show me." His fists clenched tighter against his chest.

"Perhaps I would," Orson said. He rolled his shoulders. "How about you get us started, though."

Flint remained utterly still. "I would, but then I'd have to finish. And I don't think you want me to finish you, Mr. … what's your name again?"

"I'm not listening to this anymore," Daisy muttered, turning to stomp down the stairs.

"Ooh, your words are *terrifying*," Orson said to Flint. He laughed and ran his hands up and down his arms as he pretended to shiver.

Without a word, Raven pulled Flint away. His arms fell to his sides as the two of them descended the stairs, neither of them responding to Orson's taunting words: "And there you go, letting the lady boss you around. That's no way for a man to live."

Raven marched right out of the college gates and stopped at the nearest tree. Her hand shook as she scribbled across its bark and watched a dark space open up in front of her. She picked one destination from among many in her mind and focused fully on it as she tugged Flint forward into the darkness.

On the other side of the faerie paths, they walked onto the roof of a tall building. It was night, but the winking lights that brightened the sky came from the surrounding skyscrapers, not the stars, and there was a distinct lack of magic in the air. Raven dropped her bag and began pacing, blinking away tears of fury. "You know that wasn't true, right?"

"Yes, don't worry about it."

"I mean, of course I don't mind you following me. And it's not as though you're actually *following* me. You're usually *next* to me whenever we go anywhere."

"Raven—"

"And I'd far rather hang out with you than with someone like him. You don't ruin my fun. I actually *have* fun when I'm with—"

"Raven, stop." Flint caught her shoulders and brought her to a halt. "You don't have to explain anything. I didn't believe a word he said."

She heaved out a deep breath. "Okay. Good."

Flint lowered his hands and stepped back. "He's the one you were speaking to last night at the fundraiser."

"Yes."

"The one your mother believes is a good match for you."

Raven sighed and looked past Flint to the buildings beyond. "She doesn't know what he's really like."

After a pause, Flint asked, "What happened between you two?"

Raven walked to the railing at the edge of the roof and leaned against it. "The better question would probably be, 'What happened between Orson and every other girl he ever met?'"

"Ah. I see." Flint joined her at the railing.

"He can be very charming when he wants to be, and I fell for that. He was quite the eligible young bachelor—still is, I guess—and everyone had been talking about the girl he had his eye on. Some French heiress. But then he began paying attention to me, and ... I liked it." Raven looked down and traced patterns across the metal railing with her forefinger. "I couldn't believe I was lucky enough to have caught his attention. I was dreaming about our happily ever after before he even kissed me. I was so thrilled when that kiss eventually came, but then he wanted it to remain a secret. He didn't want anyone to know about us, for reasons he would never properly explain, and he wanted me to meet him in hotel rooms, which I wasn't all that comfortable with. So after a couple of weeks of discovering that reality wasn't matching up to my dreams, I told Daisy what was going on. And guess what?" Raven smacked her hand down on the railing. "Turned out Daisy and Orson had been seeing each other in secret too—for months."

"Bastard," Flint muttered.

"Yeah. I mean, I try not to use words like that, but that's exactly what he is. He'd made all kinds of promises to Daisy, some of which he'd begun making to me too, and he clearly had no intention of keeping any of them since he was still chasing after that French girl! And though we should have been angry with Orson for his despicable behavior—and we were— Daisy and I also ended up angry with each another. Jealous, I suppose. We couldn't get past it, and we ended up not speaking for weeks. Then Orson decided to put off his work plans for a year and go traveling. With him gone, it was easier for Daisy and me to patch up our friendship. I thought things might get tense again with him being back home, but I think everything's okay." She let out a long sigh. "Anyway. Sorry. You probably didn't want to know all that."

"I asked," Flint said. "So yeah, I wanted to know. And I'm sorry. I'm glad you found out what type of person he is before things got too far." He looked down at the bright lights of the vehicles whizzing along the streets far below. "Where are we, exactly?"

Raven shrugged. "I'm not sure. I've been here a few times with my father when he needed to meet with people. I can't remember why I came with. It was long ago, so maybe he and I had been on an outing together and then he received notice of an unexpected meeting."

"He has dealings with humans?"

"Maybe. I don't know. Or maybe he was meeting faeries outside of the magic realm, for some reason." She hesitated, then shook her head slowly. "I don't even really know what my father does. How odd is that? Surely I should know and understand more? He has plenty of wealth, and he takes care of other people's wealth, and he somehow ... builds more wealth."

"Don't ask me," Flint said when she looked at him. "I haven't a clue what your dad does."

Raven's gaze traveled across the cityscape again. "Were you judging us last night?" she asked quietly. "I mean, all that unnecessary opulence on display. Did you think it was all a waste?"

"I—well—I've certainly never attended an event like that

before." He rubbed the back of neck, and she knew he wasn't saying everything on his mind. "It's just a different world, that's all. It gave me a lot to think about."

Raven nodded. "I was thinking a lot about it too." She paused, then added, "Do you ever wonder if we would have ended up friends if we'd met some other way, through day-to-day life?"

Flint's expression turned thoughtful. "I hope so. But I'm not sure how we would have met. We don't exactly move in the same circles."

"True. I often think I might prefer your circles to my circles."

"You might." He nudged her and grinned. "Although life isn't quite as easy when you're traveling in my circles."

"Hey, things aren't always easy in my circles either."

He raised an eyebrow.

"Okay, fine, so things are probably easier in my circles than in yours, but there are definitely things that suck."

"True. That black spiky delicacy you made me sample last night was indeed *ghastly*."

Raven laughed and smacked his arm. "Don't say ghastly. You sound like my mother."

His smile turned roguish. "That might have been my intention."

They watched the nighttime city buzz continue for a while, until Raven's mother sent a message to ask if she'd gone somewhere after college. They headed back through the faerie paths after that.

When dinner was done, Raven sat at her desk and sent a

message to Daisy to check if she was doing okay after their unpleasant encounter with Orson on the stairs outside Delph. Then she started piecing together the blueish grey leaves for the rest of the snake dress. When she grew tired of that, she pulled the sprite-wing dress out of her closet and got to work repairing parts of it. She'd take it back to college in the morning.

When her eyelids began to droop, she gathered up her all work and sent it, with a few swift waves of her hand, into the closet where her mother wouldn't see it if she poked her nose in here. That should be good enough. She didn't have the energy to tidy up properly.

A brief trill sounded from her amber. She flopped onto her bed and picked it up, hoping to find a reply from Daisy. Instead the glowing words on the amber's surface were written in someone else's handwriting. With her heart picking up speed, Raven read through the message three more times before jumping off her bed and heading for the door. She threw it open, calling for Flint at the same time. A figure at the other end of the passage turned, but it wasn't Flint.

"Miss Rosewood?" Rex said. "Is everything all right?"

"Um, yes, I just wanted to ask Flint something. Is he around?"

"No, his shift ended about half an hour ago. He went home."

"Oh, okay." She used to be familiar with Flint's schedule, but the whole bodyguard thing had changed that. "Thank you. I'll speak to him tomorrow."

She stepped back into her room and shut her door, chewing

her lip as she considered what to do next. Her mother would flip out if she discovered Raven was gone from the house at night without permission. But she rarely checked on Raven after dinner, so the chances were slim she'd come up here tonight.

Raven quickly changed out of her pajamas, bunched her duvet around a few scatter cushions arranged in the shape of a sleeping body, and clicked her fingers to extinguish her lamp. Then, in the near darkness, she wrote a spell for the faerie paths on her wall and walked into the black opening.

CHAPTER NINE

ALARM CROSSED FLINT'S FACE THE MOMENT HE DISCOVERED Raven outside his door. "Is something wrong?" he asked immediately, standing straighter and pulling his shoulders back.

"No, I'm fine. And you don't need to do that."

"Do what?"

"Stand like that. Like you're about to salute me or something. Just chill. You're not on duty. I'm here to show you something, that's all."

"Oh."

An awkward moment passed between them before Raven said, "So … can I come in? I mean, unless you're about to go to bed or something. I can just show you quickly and then I'll—"

"No, no, it's fine. Sorry. Come in." He stood back so she

could walk past him into the cozy living room. The smell of something chocolatey greeted her. "What do you want to show me?" He waited for her to take a seat on the nearest couch before sitting beside her.

"I received a strange message on my amber, and I wanted to show you because …" Now that she thought about it, she wasn't quite sure why she wanted to show Flint in particular. She could have taken the message to her parents, or to any one of the guards. They could easily have passed it on to the Guild for her. "Well, I just wanted to show you," she finished quickly. "Remember that scrap of paper I found on the runway? The one that made that woman come after me? I think the handwriting in this amber message was the same as the writing on that paper."

A frown creased Flint's brow. "Okay."

Raven removed a notebook from her pocket, opened it, and handed it to Flint.

"You don't have the original on your amber? So I can see the handwriting?"

"No. My amber doesn't keep messages, so I wrote it down." She frowned. "Does yours?"

"No, but I think the latest ambers do. I just assumed you'd … never mind. Where's this message?"

"You assumed I'd have one because I have the latest of everything?" Raven asked.

Flint's silence was answer enough as he flipped quickly through the pages.

"It was on the right page when I handed it to you." She took the notebook, turned to the correct page, and pushed it at him. She knew she had no right to be indignant about his comment—after all, her parents generally did buy her the latest of everything—but his assumption jabbed at her nonetheless. She crossed her arms as Flint read the message. She probably could have recited it to him, but it seemed too odd to say the words out loud.

Now that you've come so close to death, do you want to make the most of the rest of your life? You never know when it might end …

"When *it* might end?" Flint said. "'It' being your life?"

"I don't know. That's what it sounds like, right? I mean, it's a bit creepy."

"It's very creepy. Who else did you show this message to?"

"Um, no one yet. I came here first." Which suddenly felt like a silly idea when they were talking about a possible threat to her life. She probably should have gone straight to her parents or to their head of security. "But it might actually be nothing," she added. "It could be one of my classmates playing a prank." She could think of at least one person who might want to do that.

"But if it was a classmate who wrote this message, that means it was a classmate who wrote on that scrap of paper you picked up, and therefore a classmate who was involved with the explosion."

Raven paused. "True."

"Which would mean it probably isn't a prank."

"Unless I'm wrong about the handwriting."

Flint leaned forward and rested his elbows on his knees. "Well how similar did it look?"

"I can't be sure, but I think it was the same. The oversized loops on some of the letters looked the same."

"Okay. I'll definitely tell the Guild about this. And it looks like your parents probably weren't overreacting with this whole bodyguard idea." He straightened. "Hang on. Did someone accompany you here?"

"Uh, not exactly."

"Raven, you're not supposed to—"

"Please don't. You're coming very close to sounding exactly like my parents. And what is …" She sniffed the air. "What is that burning smell?"

"Oh, crap. The hot chocolate." Flint jumped up and headed for a door on the other side of the room. "Uh, I was making hot chocolate for Tora before you got here. She's up late studying for a test, and Mom isn't around to tell her to go to sleep." He turned in the doorway to face her. "Would you like some?"

"Um, yes, thank you. Can I help?"

"No, it's fine." He disappeared into the kitchen.

"Flint, who are you talking to?" came a shout from upstairs. Moments later, dragon shaped slippers appeared at the top of the stairs and began moving downward. "Oh." Flint's sister stopped when she saw Raven. "Hi."

"Hey," Raven said, giving her a small wave and trying not to feel awkward. "It's Tora, right?"

"Yeah." Tora skipped down the remaining stairs, almost tripping over her giant slippers at the same time. "Oops." She walked across the living room toward Raven, shouting, "How's that hot chocolate coming?"

"Starting again," Flint shouted back. "I kinda burned the first lot."

"Weird," Tora said, sitting on the couch across the table from Raven. "He's normally great with cooking spells. Could it be that he messed up because you're here?" she added with a sly grin.

"I—uh—what?"

Tora laughed and shook her head. "I hope he's making you some too. His hot chocolate is really great."

"So, um, you're studying for a test?" Raven asked, saying the first thing that came to mind as she attempted to regain her composure.

"Yes. The use of transformation magic in defense."

"Oh, are you a guardian too?"

Tora nodded. "Well, I'm a trainee. I'm in my second year."

Raven tucked her legs beneath her and hugged one of the cushions against her chest. "So you and Flint, and your dad …" She paused for a moment, hesitant to speak about a father who had passed away. "Is it a family thing? Is your mom a guardian too?"

"Oh, goodness, no. I can't image that." Tora pushed one hand through her hair. "She's a healer. Sometimes she works night shifts, which is why she isn't here tonight."

"Okay. Does she work at the Guild's healing institute?"

"No, she's at that little place on the edge of Creepy Hollow. Old and kinda rundown. They get a lot of Undergrounders there, so if you're a faerie and you're sick, you'd probably go somewhere else."

Raven nodded, not wanting to admit she'd never heard of that particular healing center, or that her parents would never visit a place like that. It made her feel uncomfortable in the same way Flint's assumption about her owning the best of everything made her uncomfortable. "Tora," she said, scooting forward a little on the couch. "Does Flint ... does he think that I'm ... I'm a spoiled brat?"

Tora's eyes widened in surprise, but her laugh soon caught up. "I don't think so. I know all the things he *does* think of you, and 'spoiled brat' doesn't seem to fit in there."

It was Raven's turn to be surprised. "He's spoken about me?"

"Of course. In the beginning he was so bored with his new job that he told us about anything remotely interesting that ever happened. 'A goblin climbed over the wall this morning,' or 'Mrs Rosewood tripped on her way out of the house,' or 'I almost tied up this pretty girl because I thought she was an intruder,' or—" Tora paused with her mouth open, her cheeks growing slowly pinker. "But—um—you should probably pretend I never said any of those things, since Flint would kill me if he knew."

"If I knew what?" Flint asked, walking back into the room while carefully directing three mugs through the air in front of him.

"Nothing," Tora said, far too quickly.

He lowered the mugs to the coffee table before fixing Tora with a frown. "What did you tell Raven?"

Raven spoke up before Tora could implicate herself further.

"Nothing important." She smiled sweetly. "Only good things." Like the fact that he'd told his family she was pretty.

"Good things that would make me want to kill Tora if I knew about them?" Flint asked. "Now that I definitely don't believe."

"She told me you make amazing hot chocolate, so I'm looking forward to finding out if that's true." Raven placed the cushion she'd been hugging on her lap and held her hands out for a mug, hoping Flint would be happy with the change of subject. He sighed, then picked up a mug and passed it to her. "Oh, what is that?" she exclaimed in delight as a cloud of gold dust that smelled like cinnamon rose from the top of the chocolate liquid and coalesced into a miniature unicorn. It danced across the top of her drink before diving into the liquid with the tiniest of splashes and disappearing. "That's amazing. How did you do that?"

A self-satisfied smile spread across his face as he sat beside her. "I have my secret spells."

"And wait till you taste it," Tora added. "You'll love it."

"Thank you, Tora," Flint said, his tone a bit sterner now, "but you should either be studying or sleeping."

"But I wanted to ask Raven about fashion school."

"You'll have to ask her another time."

"Ooh, you'll be visiting again?" Tora asked Raven.

"Um, I … I hope so." She cast a questioning glance at Flint, but he was taking a sip of his hot chocolate.

"Fine, okay, we can talk next time." Tora reached for her mug and headed for the stairs with it.

"I like her," Raven said quietly.

Flint rolled his eyes and chuckled. "Anyway, do you like it?" He motioned to the mug in her hands.

She brought it to her lips and took a sip. It was so rich and delectable she almost melted into the couch. Instead, she nodded. "Absolutely. Tora was right. I think you need to teach Aunty Sweetpea this recipe."

He shook his head. "This one's my secret."

Raven drank again, a larger sip this time, before lowering the mug. "What does your guard duty consist of now when you aren't with me? Do you patrol the house?

"I patrol the inside of the house—I'm not stationed outside anymore—and remain alert for potential damsel-in-distress screams."

Raven rolled her eyes. "That must get so boring."

"Fortunately it's a large and interesting house."

She leaned back and wrapped both hands around the mug. "Seriously, though. You probably want to lose your mind from the monotony of walking around the same place all the time."

"Is that what Tora told you?"

"Stop worrying about whatever Tora told me. She didn't need to say a word for me to figure out that your job is boring."

"It isn't too bad."

Raven gave him a knowing look. "Now that's a lie."

"Look, it isn't all that bad. In fact, it recently got far more interesting when I was assigned as personal bodyguard to my employers' daughter instead of the garden or the entrance or the wall."

"While I find that very flattering—" she batted her eyelashes at him "—don't you miss working at a Guild?"

"I …" His gaze fell away from hers. "I do."

"Why did you leave?"

"I needed a break. Well, *the Guild* decided I needed a break."

"What happened?"

Flint settled back in his chair. "I was undercover for almost a year, very involved with a few members of the Unseelie Court. Centuries old, some of them, dealing in ancient spells, dark magic, and … other things. I was probably far too young and inexperienced for so lengthy and dangerous an assignment, but circumstances at the time led to me being the right person for the job. In the end, after the whole operation went south, I wound up in the healing wing for almost a week. After that, the Guild suggested I take a break for a while. Do something different for a few years. That's how I ended up in private security, since I still wanted to protect people, of course."

Raven sat for several moments trying to figure out what to say. "That's … wow. I'm so glad you survived."

"Me too." He chuckled. "Obviously."

"It's just …" She paused and shook her head. "How can you stand to be around people like me?"

Confusion crossed his features. "What?"

"My life—my parents and friends and my work—it's all so superficial and meaningless. You saved lives, fought dangerous creatures, and submerged yourself in a deadly world to bring down evil—and now you're stuck walking around the homes of rich people. It must drive you crazy."

"Raven, people need to wear clothes. Your work might not

seem as thrilling, but it isn't meaningless."

"Half the things I create would never be worn by any ordinary person on any ordinary day." She placed her mug on the coffee table and hugged the cushion again. "I should be casting clothes that are more sensible. Maybe that would help more people. No one needs all those frivolous outfits I'm always coming up with. I could tone down on—"

"Hey." He leaned over and took her hand. "Sometimes people need frivolous in their lives. And that creativity is part of who you are. Don't tone it down. I'm serious, Raven. You can't be ashamed of the thing you're most passionate about. You just have to find the best way to use it, that's all."

Raven's eyes flicked down to their joined hands. Heat began to spread out from somewhere deep inside her. She didn't want him to let go. She wanted to slide her fingers between his. She wanted to feel the rough skin of his palms—

Flint pulled his hand back just as a crash resounded from the direction of the kitchen.

"What was that?" Raven asked.

"Probably nothing," he said quickly.

"Oh. Are you sure?"

"Yeah, I'm sure everything's fine. You should—"

"—probably go. I know. But you'll take that message—"

"—to the Guild, yes. In fact, I'll contact a friend of mine right now. He might even be there tonight, so he can pass the message on immediately."

"Okay, thanks."

"You'll go straight home from here?" Flint asked.

"Yes. Straight into my bedroom. Wouldn't want my parents to catch me coming home now."

"Definitely not. And Raven," he added. "Please don't forget what I said. Your work can still add value to people's lives."

She nodded as she turned to leave. "Thanks, Flint."

CHAPTER TEN

SEVEN. THAT WAS THE GLOWING BLUE NUMBER THAT floated above Raven's desk on this fine Friday morning. She would rather have been making plans with Daisy to lie outside in the sun this afternoon, but with the final show only a week away, she'd have to keep working all afternoon. Especially since she wouldn't be able to continue into the evening because of that silly flower casters' party she was hosting with her mother tonight.

Raven had thought a lot about Flint's words over the past few days. She decided it probably was possible to use clothes casting in a way that benefited others, although she hadn't yet figured out anything specific. But being a good hostess at a ball for the local flower casters society? She wasn't sure how worthwhile a skill that was.

Racing to college and just about gluing her butt to a chair all day, she managed to get a lot done. Joining all the leaves together for the snake dress was time-consuming work, but she managed to get a good portion of it completed, as well as the delicate metal band she'd decided should go around the model's head.

"How was Von Milta Madness?" Cecilia asked Raven when she popped in briefly at the end of the day to see how a few of the last-minute outfits were going. "You had some pieces on show this year, didn't you?"

"Yes, it was lots of fun. I hope I get invited to take part again some time in the future." All the Madness outfits had been auctioned off for charity, which Raven excitedly pointed out to Flint when she realized that might be the first tiny bit of good her fashion skills had brought about. She couldn't count on being invited to Von Milta Madness every year, though, so she'd have to come up with another worthy cause for her future. Something that hopefully wouldn't clash with the internship she was so desperate to get …

"Wonderful," Cecilia said. "And you seem to be moving along quickly with this piece." She examined some of the leaves, gave Raven a few helpful hints—which Raven hurriedly scribbled down in her notebook—and added, "You might even have time to work on fixing the sprite-wing dress before the final show."

"I started on that last night, actually, since I had it at home. But it's back there now with the rest of my collection." She motioned to the room behind her where all the finished pieces were stored. Each student's section of the room was sealed off from the others with an enchantment. An unnecessary safeguard most of the time, but students had been known to sabotage each other's work in the past. With people like Bella hanging around, Raven was grateful for the precaution.

After college, Raven took parts of the new dress home with her and worked on them until her mother appeared in her bedroom doorway, wanting to know why she wasn't ready yet. "You're supposed to be inspecting the decor downstairs with me now."

"Oh. Is it possible there's something wrong with it?"

"I certainly hope not, but we need to check it anyway. We're entertaining flower casters, after all, so the flower arrangements need to be spectacular."

"Well, can I come down when I'm dressed?"

Zalea heaved a frustrated sigh. "Fine. Please hurry up."

Raven picked out a pink dress with a puffy skirt and flower embellishments weaving their way up her back and over her shoulders. It seemed appropriate for the occasion. She tidied her notebooks, bending quickly to pick one up that had fallen. She was about to close it and drop it onto the pile when she noticed the writing next to one of her older unused designs. *Too much fluffy girliness for the assigned theme*, read the note. It wasn't the words themselves that had caught her attention, but how they were written: in a larger, cleaner script than her own, with looping Fs, Ys and Gs.

With her heart pounding faster, she paged through the rest of the notebook. Then she looked through all the others, searching for the same handwriting, hoping to find a clue as to who it belonged to. But she couldn't find it anywhere else.

She ran on bare feet to her door and tugged it open, then peered down the passage to see if the figure at the other end was her bodyguard or someone else. "Flint?" she called.

He looked around. "Yes? Do you need something?"

She motioned with her hand for him to come closer. "Look here," she said when he stopped in front of her. "This is the handwriting. The same as the scrap of paper I picked up, and the same as that amber message I received."

He took the notebook from her hands and examined the writing. "Do you know who it belongs to?"

"No. And I can't find it in any of my other books. It must be someone I've hardly ever worked with."

"Can I take this?" He waved the notebook.

"Um …" Raven thought for a moment. "Yes. It's an older one. I don't need anything that's in it."

"Okay, I'll drop it off at the Guild just now when my shift ends."

"Oh, you're not staying tonight?" Disappointment settled over her.

"No, I requested this evening off a while ago. It's—"

"Tora's birthday. Of course. You told me about it weeks ago, before I even met her." She shook her head and walked to the vanity. "I made her something, and then with the explosion and the intruder and everything, I completely forgot about it. I'm so sorry." She removed a small box from the top drawer of the vanity and handed it to Flint. "Now that I know she's a guardian trainee, I might not have chosen to make jewelry. She probably doesn't have much occasion to wear it."

"She likes jewelry, though," Flint said, "even if she doesn't wear it that often. I'm sure she'll love whatever you've made her."

"Okay." Raven gave him a shy smile. "Great."

"Enjoy your party tonight."

Her shoulders drooped. "Ugh. I wish I was going to the party you're going to instead."

"Maybe next time. Tora would love that."

* * *

"Mom, what is Orson doing here?" The party was in full swing, with plenty of giggling, drinking and entertainment going on, and the last person Raven wanted to see had just walked in.

Zalea blinked at her daughter in momentary confusion. "He was invited, of course. What's wrong with having him here? He's a friend of yours."

"He isn't, actually."

"Oh. Well you two can become friends tonight then. But remember to talk to as many people as possible. That's part of being a good hostess. We want *everyone* to feel welcome."

Raven almost rolled her eyes. Hosting parties was fun, of course, but she'd far rather host one for ten people than a hundred. "Yes, Mom," she said with a sigh.

"Have you spoken to Marigold yet? She's over there with her daughters. Go and tell them all how lovely they look."

Raven followed her mother's instructions and chatted politely with Marigold and her daughters. After several minutes had passed, she excused herself to move on to the next person.

She was distracted, however, by Orson laughing loudly with one of the waitresses. She stopped beside him. "Good evening, Orson. It looks like you're having a lot of fun, but I think it might be better if you leave."

"Hm. My mother's part of the flower casters society, though. I'm pretty sure I saw my name on the guest list."

"That was an unfortunate mistake."

"It's okay, we can meet up later," the waitress said to Orson with a wink.

Orson returned the wink and smacked the waitress's backside as she headed away.

"Don't be so vulgar," Raven hissed.

"What? My hand just slipped."

Without pause, she stamped her heel down hard on top of his shoe. As he cried out and swore at her, she said, "What? I guess my foot just slipped."

A strong hand with long nails gripped Raven's upper arm and pulled her away from Orson. "How dare you behave like that toward one of our guests?" Zalea whispered furiously. She tugged Raven across the room and out the door. In the entrance hall behind one of the large flower arrangements, she finally let go of Raven. "What is wrong with you? You're not a child anymore. Okay, so you're not interested in Orson. That doesn't mean you have to physically assault him."

"Mom, you have no idea what a scumbag he is. The things he's done and said and lied about—"

"He isn't a scumbag. He's the son of—"

"You don't know him, Mom!" Raven said, clutching her mother's shoulders. "You don't know *anything* about what happened with him and me, or with him and Daisy, or the countless other girls he's tried to seduce."

"To seduce?" Zalea looked at her as though she were speaking a foreign language. "What are you talking about?"

"He ..." She swallowed. "He tries to convince girls to enter into secret relationships with him. It happened to me—and to Daisy—before he went away for a year."

Finally, an appropriate amount of horror began to make its way onto Zalea's face. "Did he—"

"Nothing actually happened. Nothing much, anyway. But Daisy's worried about having her reputation ruined, so please don't say anything about her being involved."

"I can't believe you didn't tell me about this when it happened."

"Because I felt so stupid that I'd been taken in by his charm. And it was over anyway, so what would have been the point?"

Zalea folded her arms and tapped her foot. "Well. Okay. We shall make sure Orson Willowstack is asked to leave the party immediately. Quietly, of course. We don't want to cause a scene. Then you and I will go back out there and make sure our guests are having the most wonderful time. You can forget all about Orson and enjoy the rest of the evening. You might even meet some other wonderful young man."

Raven stood a steadying breath. "No."

"Excuse me?"

"I don't want to do this. *Any* of this. I don't want to host huge parties, and I don't want to *not* make a scene about Orson. Don't you think people need to know what kind of person he is? So at the very least they can all warn their daughters away from him?"

"Yes," Zalea said, "but that revelation will not be happening at any party of mine. Can you imagine the scandal? I don't want to be linked to something like that."

Raven shook her head in disbelief. "Are you really so selfish?"

"No, Raven, I'm smart. A trait I had hoped to pass on to you."

"Well if this is the kind of smart you're talking about, then I'm afraid you failed." She tugged her long skirt up and swept past her mother.

CHAPTER ELEVEN

AFTER PACING FOR A WHILE ACROSS HER BEDROOM, RAVEN changed into the plainest clothes she could find in her closet: blank pants and a pale blue fitted T-shirt. She was certain it was the only T-shirt she owned. She'd never bought or made one, so someone must have given it to her. She couldn't remember the occasion, though.

She didn't want to stay here. She didn't want to go to Daisy's either. She wanted to see Flint, and it struck her suddenly that these days, he was always the one she wanted to see. But Flint had other plans tonight, and she didn't want to mess with that. Still … perhaps she could message him about meeting up later.

She picked up her amber, held her stylus above its surface, and realized she'd never sent Flint a message before. She'd never needed to. Before she could ponder whether she was crossing some sort of line she hadn't previously noticed, she wrote her message onto the amber. As long as she focused hard enough on him while writing it, it should find its intended destination.

Hi. I know you're at Tora's party, but do you want to go out somewhere afterwards? Raven

Then she sat on the edge of her bed and waited, chewing her lip instead of chewing her nails. A few minutes passed before a faint jingle alerted her to Flint's reply.

We're almost finished. Wasn't really a party. Just birthday dinner with family. She's partying with her friends tomorrow night. Where do you want to go?

Anywhere as long as it's far away from the party currently happening here.

Right. Got it. I'm guessing you won't be bringing a guard with you then. Meet me at my place in fifteen minutes? I'll wait outside for you.

Raven was starting to feel better already. She watched the enchanted hourglass beside her bed until about thirteen minutes had passed. Then she switched her lamp off without bothering to arrange any cushions beneath her duvet. If her mother wanted to come in here and check up on her, then she'd find an empty bedroom. Raven was already in trouble for refusing to go back into the party, so why not add another broken rule to the mix?

She walked into the faerie paths and pictured the inside of Flint's home. Since she obviously didn't have access to it, the faerie paths brought her out beside his tree. He was waiting for her, leaning in the doorway and staring into the dark, overgrown forest. "Hey," he said when he saw her. He straightened and smiled, and the tension instantly melted from Raven's body. She didn't know at what point he'd become her anchor, her calming influence, but there was no denying it.

"You look different," he said.

"I know, it's super plain and boring." She pulled at the hem of her T-shirt. "All of a sudden I just didn't want to stand out anymore."

"No, I didn't mean plain or boring. You look nice."

She rolled her eyes. "You always say that, no matter what I'm wearing."

"I always mean it."

"He does always mean it," Tora shouted from inside the house. "He always tells us how—"

Flint swept his hand quickly through the air, sending a snowball flying into the house. Tora's squeal a second later told Raven the snowball had struck its intended target. Flint gave her a guilty grin. "She talks too much sometimes. Want to come inside before we choose somewhere to go?"

Raven stepped into the house. "Happy birthday," she said to Tora, who was lying on the couch with a book.

"Thanks. Oh, thank you for the bracelet ring thing." She

sat up quickly. "I don't even know what to call it, but it's so cool."

Raven pictured the bracelet of silver leaves and the silver pieces that trailed down the back of the hand and connected to a silver ring on each finger. "You're welcome. I hope you find an occasion to wear it sometime."

"I wore it tonight. We went out to a nice restaurant, and my dress had silver elements on it, so I figured it kind of matched. Actually, I just wanted to wear it, so it wouldn't have mattered what dress I had on," she added with a laugh.

"I'm so glad," Raven said, perching on the arm of the couch.

"Do you mind if I call a friend quickly?" Flint said, holding up a mirror. "We were going to go out this evening, so I just—"

"Oh, I'm so sorry." Raven stood. "That's fine. I didn't mean to interrupt your plans. I'll see you tomorrow at—"

"No, no, you can come with us," Flint said. "I mean, if you want to. It's just a few of us hanging out."

"Okay, well if I'm not imposing ..."

"You won't be." Flint left the room, and Raven sat on the couch arm again. She was about to ask Tora what book she was reading when Flint's mother walked into the room. Flint must have warned her that Raven would be stopping by, because she didn't seem surprised.

"Hello, Raven," she said. "It's nice to see you again." She seemed reserved, though, so Raven couldn't quite tell if she meant it or not.

"Hi ..." Darn it, how did she still not know Flint's surname? It was so rude of her not to address his mother by name. "I'm sorry for intruding on Tora's birthday," she added quickly.

"Why are you sorry?" Tora asked. "Birthdays are for celebrating, not for hiding away from people. It's totally fine that you're here. Besides, you gave me a birthday present. Can't really shut you out after that, can I?"

"Tora, don't be rude," her mother murmured.

"It's fine," Raven said with a laugh. Flint's mother gave her a polite smile before heading for the stairs, leaving Raven feeling as though she should have done more or said more to prove that she was worthy of hanging out with an amazing guy like Flint.

"You really don't have to feel weird about being here," Tora said, probably reading Raven's uncertain expression. "I'm happy you came back. I like you a lot more than the other girl Flint brought home."

Raven was surprised by the flash of jealousy that heated her veins. "What other girl?"

"Oh, it was a while ago, don't worry." Raven placed her book on the cushion next to her and crossed her legs. "It was during his last year as a trainee at the Guild. She was in his class. I didn't mind her when she was just Flint's friend, but as his girlfriend she was bossy and possessive. And Flint is polite, but he isn't a doormat, so he didn't appreciate being bossed around. I mean, who would? So anyway, they fought a lot, and he finally broke up with her when he started working at the Guild after he graduated." She smiled at Raven. "You seem much nicer than her."

"Well, thank you." Raven's face warmed. "But, you know,

it isn't like that. He works for my parents, and we're just …
sort of … friends. Although my parents don't know that part."
She frowned. "It's a bit weird, I guess. Not a normal kind of
friendship."

"Yeah …" Tora drew the word out, giving Raven a
doubtful look. "Definitely not just friendship."

"Shall we go?" Flint asked, coming down the stairs two at a
time.

"Yes." Raven stood up. "Where are we going?"

"Karaoke."

Raven frowned. "What's that?"

"It's quite lame, actually, but I have these two friends who
are really into it. It's kind of an entertainment form in the
human realm. They play instrumental versions of popular
songs, and the words come up on a TV screen. You get on
stage and sing along into a microphone." He paused. "You
know what a TV is, right?"

"Yes, Flint. I may not hang out on the non-magical side of
the veil all that often, but I'm aware of the box known as the
television."

"How about a microphone?"

She bit her lip. "Okay, so I'm less familiar with that one."

"No problem." Flint grinned. "We'll soon get you well
acquainted."

* * *

Raven had close to zero talent in the singing department, but
that didn't stop her from getting on stage and embarrassing

herself in front of a half-empty bar—and loving every minute of it. Flint had a go, and he was actually quite good. Raven clapped and hugged him when he returned to their table, then pulled away quickly when she realized it was the first time she'd ever hugged him. It was strange. Strange, yet something she wanted to repeat very soon, if possible.

When one of his friends got up to sing for the third time, Flint asked Raven if she wanted to get some fresh air. "There are some stairs back there leading to the roof." He motioned over his shoulder.

"Yeah, that would nice. It's a bit stuffy in here."

They climbed the rickety metal steps and walked through the half-open door onto the roof. It wasn't nearly as high as the skyscraper they'd been on top of a few nights before, and the surrounding area was a little run-down, but Raven didn't mind. She didn't think she'd mind any setting as long as Flint was standing next to her.

"What went wrong at the party tonight?" he asked. "You left far too early for it to have been over."

Raven stood on tiptoe and peered over the wall at the street below, trying to decide how to explain herself. She leaned against the wall and looked at him. "First it was everything, and then it was Orson, and then it was everything all over again. I just didn't want to be there anymore."

"How mad was your mother?"

Raven let out a humorless laugh. "I think I embarrassed her dreadfully by leaving the party early. Although, knowing my mother, she probably made up an excuse for my absence. Perhaps she told everyone I wasn't feeling well." She sighed.

"It's just … it all feels like a silly game sometimes. You dress up and say all the right things to the right people at the right time, and for what? Mom seems to enjoy it, but I don't. I'd rather have a handful of *real* friends and hang out with them."

Flint nodded. "I think I have to agree with you on that one."

"Anyway, let's talk about something else."

"Okay. Have you received any other strange amber messages?"

"No, nothing else. Have you heard anything from the Guild about who the handwriting in my notebook might belong to?"

"I don't know details, but I think they're still looking through samples of handwriting from everyone at Delphinium College. It isn't a particularly promising lead, though, since there's no way of proving that the owner of a piece of handwriting in your notebook had anything to do with the explosion."

"But it's at least somewhere to start, right?"

"Yes, I suppose so. They can question the person if they find him or her."

A breeze drifted by, lifting the ends of Raven's hair and raising goosebumps on her bare arms. "Flint, does your mother not like me?"

Confusion crossed Flint's features. "What?"

"I mean, is she maybe still upset about when we arrived in the middle of the night and woke her and Tora?"

"No, why?"

"I just get the feeling she doesn't like me."

"She does like you. She thinks you're lovely."

"Really? But she seemed very ... careful? Distanced? I don't know. Just not particularly warm toward me."

"That's just ... because ..." Flint shook his head, his cheeks flushing. "It doesn't matter. It's just a silly thing."

"What silly thing?"

"Look, she does like you, okay? You haven't done anything to offend her."

"Okay." Raven wished he'd explain further, but she decided not to press him. She ran her hands up and down her arms, chasing the goosebumps away.

Flint removed the hoodie draped over his shoulders and offered it to her. "I'm sure it'll be far too big on you, but at least you won't be cold."

"Thanks." Her heart jolted into a faster rhythm as she took the hoodie from him and pulled it over her head. If she hadn't crossed a line earlier when she messaged him, she was certainly crossing one now by wearing his clothes. To be honest, though, they'd probably crossed the line of propriety a year ago when they decided to keep meeting every week on the tower. She pushed the long sleeves up to reveal her hands and tried to act normal, though she was beginning to feel anything but. "I don't think I've ever worn a hoodie before."

"Yeah, it doesn't quite fit in with the rest of your wardrobe, does it."

"I like it. It's comfortable." And it smelled like him, though she hadn't realized until now that this precise scent, something warm and spicy, was a scent she associated solely with Flint.

She looked around the rooftop at the rickety old bench and

the flowerpots filled with overgrown plants. "I think roofs are our thing. We always end up on one. The tower at home, the skyscraper, this old building."

He looked at her, a hint of a smile on his lips as he said, "I didn't realize we had a thing."

She played with the sleeves of the hoodie as she focused somewhere on the region of his chest, too self-conscious now to meet his eyes. "I think you have realized we have a … thing."

"I'm getting the feeling," he said softly, "that you're not referring to roofs anymore."

She bit her lip and shook her head. "I'm not."

He reached for her hand and slowly wove his fingers between hers, sending more goosebumps racing up her arms. "I don't know what—or how—I just wish I …" He shook his head and took a deep breath. "I wish I wasn't in the position I'm in. It just … complicates things."

Raven finally managed to look up and meet his eyes. "Can't I just be me and you be you? Without my family and your position and all the extra stuff that makes this complicated?"

"I don't know. Can we?"

She raised her hand and placed it carefully on his chest. She felt the steady pounding of his heart. "Yes."

Flint's eyes traveled across her face and down to her lips as he leaned—

An unexpected crack and crunch startled them both, followed by the door slamming shut and a spiral of sparks zipping its way around the bench. The bench that now sloped down on the right due to two of its legs having snapped in half.

"Oh, that's so embarrassing," Raven said with a giggle. She covered her blushing face with her hands. "I wish magic didn't make it so hard to hide one's emotions."

Flint gently pulled her hands away from her face. A smile stretched at his lips. "Why would you want to hide anything from me? And hey, maybe it was my uncontrolled magic that escaped, not yours."

Raven released a breathless laugh as she watched tiny sparks escaping their joined hands. "Pretty sure it was mine."

"I think," Flint said, leaning closer, "it's actually both of us."

He kissed her, softly, carefully, and in a way that made her desperate for more. He released her hands and spread his fingers through her hair. Her arms, which she seemed to have no control over anymore, slid around his back. She breathed him in, pressed herself closer, and her skin, her lips, her tongue—everything tingled with magic. Sirens could have raced by on the road below and she wouldn't have heard them. The sky could have cracked open and released a deluge, and she wouldn't have felt a thing but Flint's hands and his breath and his heart beat and the sparks he trailed across her skin.

She never wanted it to end.

CHAPTER TWELVE

SHE WAS IN SO MUCH TROUBLE THE FOLLOWING MORNING. Her mother came into her room and shouted up a storm before Raven had even climbed out of bed. Admittedly, it wasn't exactly early. She'd stayed in bed far longer than usual, half awake and dreaming of Flint. Then her mother had thrown the door open and ruined her reverie.

"You can't go running off like that in the middle of the night without a guard. What if you had been killed out there? I didn't get a moment of sleep until Rex informed us you'd returned."

"How would I have been killed, Mom? I was just hanging out in the human realm, that's all."

"The human realm? That's even worse! How would we have found you if something had happened?"

Raven covered her face and groaned. "Nothing happened."

"And nothing *will* be happening. You're finishing your outfits, going to college, and that's it. Nowhere else."

"Mom—"

"Nowhere!"

"Do you realize you're trying to ground an eighteen year old who will very soon be graduating and possibly moving out?"

"*Moving out?*" Zalea looked at her in disbelief. Then she shook her head and started laughing. "What nonsense. Where would you go?" She continued laughing as she marched out of the room. "You should have been here last night," she snapped to someone in the passage. "You could have stopped her from running off and doing whatever wild and dangerous things she was getting up to."

Was that Flint her mother was talking to? Raven leaned to the side and tried to see out the door, but Zalea slammed it shut. She ran her fingers through her mussed up hair, unable to contain the smile spreading across her face. If Flint was here, it didn't matter how long she was grounded for. He was the only one she wanted to see. Even if she spent all day in her bedroom working on her dress, while Flint patrolled the house and the passage outside her room, talking to her through the open door, she'd be happy.

She floated in the pool in her bathing room for a while, enjoying the hot waterfall that cascaded over a rock display and onto her shoulders. When she went downstairs for breakfast, Flint wasn't outside her room. She kept an eye out for him while eating, but he must have been in another part of the house. Returning upstairs, though, she found him standing near her door. She almost ran toward him, but managed to restrict herself to a normal walking pace. She couldn't keep the smile from her lips, though. "Hi," she said, stopping in front of him.

"Good morning, Miss Rosewood."

"Apparently you should have been here last night to stop me from doing something wild and dangerous."

Flint cleared his throat and made an admirable effort at keeping a straight face. "Thank goodness I wasn't."

"Thank goodness, indeed." She pressed her lips together and forced herself not to laugh as she walked past him into her bedroom. "Do you mind checking the door to my balcony? It feels like it's got stuck, and I can't come up with the right spell to open it."

"Uh, certainly." Flint looked anything but certain, though, as he walked into Raven's bedroom. He crossed the floor to the balcony doors and opened them easily, because of course there was nothing wrong with them. "Look at that," he said. "Must be my magic touch."

Raven stifled a giggle and moved closer to him. She took his hand. "I had fun last night. The singing, and meeting your friends, and then ..." She blushed. "Obviously everything on the roof."

Flint looked over her shoulder, then bent quickly and kissed her. "I don't know how we're supposed to make this work," he whispered, "but we can figure it out." He kissed her again. "I don't want to let you go."

She wrapped her arms around him and rested her head against his chest. "You don't have to."

He left her room soon after that, and she got to work on more of the leaves for the snake dress. Hopefully, by the end of the weekend, she could begin putting the whole thing together. Then she could ask the model to come in for a fitting on Tuesday, and she'd be finished just in time for Friday's show.

Zalea poked her head into the room several times during the day to check that Raven was working hard and hadn't disappeared again. She mentioned that someone would be there the following day to adjust the faerie paths access magic so that Raven could no longer travel anywhere from inside her bedroom. Raven said nothing, knowing that if she wanted to leave badly enough, she'd simply do it from somewhere else in the house.

Sunday continued in the same way, with Raven on her bedroom floor surrounded by leaves, jewels and scattered notebooks, and with Flint stopping by every hour to talk to her. By the time she climbed into bed that evening, she was ready to put the dress together the next day. The process would involve quite a few spells she needed to get absolutely right, so a good night's sleep was probably important.

But it took a while before she drifted off to sleep. Thoughts of Flint filled her mind, making her smile into her pillow. She'd never looked forward to a Monday as much as she did tonight. She craved the feeling of his arms around her, and it would be a whole lot easier to spend time alone with him in the grounds outside the college than at home with her parents nearby. Raven knew she'd have to tell them eventually and deal with their unpleasant reactions, but for now she would enjoy her happiness.

CHAPTER THIRTEEN

"SO YOU'VE FINISHED?" FLINT ASKED ON MONDAY AFTER-
noon. "It's all done?" He pulled her closer and placed a kiss on
her forehead.

"Almost. The model's coming tomorrow, so I'll do final
adjustments after she tries it on. But yes, then it will done. So
I'll have two days to make sure the rest of my pieces are still
looking good, and I'll be ready for Friday."

"Perfect."

They were in the trees outside the college walls, far enough
away that no one would see them. They only had about
another ten minutes before Flint would be in trouble for not
bringing Raven home straight after college.

"I've been thinking about us," he said slowly, "and … it
doesn't feel quite right."

She went still in his arms, a chill running through her. "What do you mean?"

"I don't mean being with you. That feels more right than anything. I mean being with you in secret without your parents knowing. It doesn't feel like the honorable thing to do."

"I know, but what's the alternative?"

"We could tell them."

She laughed. "Tell them? Are you serious? You know how they'll react."

"Yes, but ... you're their daughter. If this is what makes you happy, why can't they be happy too?"

"Because ..." Raven sighed. "Because they think they know better than I do about what will make me happy."

His fingers slowly traced her spine from the top of her neck down to the small of her back. "Is that the only reason you don't want our relationship to be public?"

"Yes. What other reason could there be?"

"Perhaps you're ... ashamed to be with someone like me?"

"What?" She stepped back. "Where did that come from?"

"Would you really be proud to stand beside me in front of all your friends and all your parents' friends, with everyone knowing that you're an heiress to a fortune, and I'm just the guy who guards the front door?"

It probably wasn't a good time to point out that he guarded more than the front door these days, so she decided not to mention that. "Of course I'd be proud to stand beside you."

"And yet we're hiding in the forest right now, because it isn't just your parents we're keeping this from, it's everyone."

"Yes, because Delph is filled with people who can't keep

their mouths shut, and the news would reach my mother before we even get home." She placed her hands gently on either side of his face. "I want to be with you, Flint, no matter how difficult it might end up being."

"So you don't care what people think?"

She pushed aside the niggling doubt at the back of her mind, the part of her that wanted to avoid the whispers and judgment and keep this special thing just between the two of them. "No. I don't care."

"Then I stand by what I said just now." He took her hands and held them both, squeezing them briefly. "We need to tell your parents. Perhaps not today or this week, but very soon."

"After graduation on Saturday," she said. "I'll know by then if I've won the internship. My parents' moods will greatly depend on whether I get it or not, but we'll tell them either way. Okay?"

Flint nodded, looking happier. "Okay."

They walked out of the faerie paths into the entrance hall at home and parted ways on the stairs.

"Stop."

Raven looked back at the sound of her mother's voice. Zalea walked out of the dining room and stood in the center of the entrance hall. She folded her arms across her chest and looked first at Raven, then at Flint.

Raven stepped back down and stood beside him. "Yes? Is something wrong?"

"Something is most definitely wrong." Zalea's jaw tensed before she continued. "I am shocked, utterly appalled, and extremely disappointed, Raven."

"Mom, what are you—"

"I know about the two of you," she shouted. Her eyes flashed back and forth between Raven and Flint. "Someone in the garden looked up and saw you together on your balcony this morning in an embrace far more intimate than should ever be appropriate between a lady and her guard."

Raven raised her hands in an attempt to placate her mother. "I was planning to tell you about us—"

"That doesn't make it any better!" her mother fumed.

"I think I should probably leave," Flint said quietly.

"You most certainly will leave. And don't even think about coming back. Consider yourself fired."

"Mom—"

"Stop talking." Zalea looked at Flint. "I will make certain you never get a job anywhere else after you've broken our trust and behaved so improperly. Now get out." Flint exchanged a brief look with Raven before turning and leaving through the front door. Zalea focused on her daughter. "How could you do something like this?"

"*Me?*" Raven blinked back angry tears. "How could *you* speak to Flint like that?"

"I will speak to him however I choose after what he's done." She shook her bangles and began pacing. "And you had the nerve to tell me *Orson* is the one trying to seduce young ladies."

"OH MY GOODNESS. Flint is a hundred times the man Orson is. He's been nothing but decent since the day I met him a *year* ago. We've been friends ever since—which you knew nothing about, of course—and he's never done anything inappropriate. We couldn't help falling for one another, and guess what? *He* was the one who wanted to tell you and Dad about us. Not me. Because I knew you'd react like this."

"Of course I'm reacting this way." Zalea sighed and ceased her pacing. "Raven, you need to think. Just *think*. Where can this possibly go? You can't form a union with someone like him."

"No one said anything about getting married!" Raven yelled. "You have heard of dating, right?"

"And what is the point of dating if not with a consideration for a potential union? And if you *don't* see him as potential union material, then what are you getting so upset about?"

"I *do* see him as union material, I'm just saying that no one's talking about getting married *now*."

"I'm afraid you won't ever be marrying someone like him."

Raven groaned and turned for the stairs. "This is pointless. Absolutely pointless. If you can't accept him, then you can't accept me. At the end of the week, when graduation is done, I'm leaving."

"Raven!" Her mother shouted after her. "You're really going to give up all of this—everything this family can offer you—for a boy?"

"I'm not giving this up for a boy! I'm giving it up for a principle."

Zalea slowly shook her head. "No. This isn't about principles. Do you really think we'd be in this position, with you threatening to run away, if you hadn't fallen in love with someone completely inappropriate?"

"Probably not. But it would have happened at some stage. There's so much about the way we live that I don't agree with.

If we didn't clash over my choice of boyfriend or husband, we'd soon be clashing over something else. So yes, this is about principles."

"Fine then." Zalea lifted her chin. "If these principles are so important to you, then you'll leave right now."

"What?"

"No need to wait until after graduation. You might as well get out of the house now. And since you're so unhappy with our way of life, I assume you won't need to take any of the many things we've bought you."

"What do you—"

"You can take the bag you're carrying. That's it."

Raven ground her teeth together. "But there are things upstairs that I need for the final show. Items I stored at home instead of at Delph."

"Well, that's unfortunate."

Raven swiped at a tear that managed to escape. "Why don't you just come out and say it, Mom: Flint or my career."

"Fine. Flint or your career. It's your choice."

More tears burned their way down her cheeks as she attempted to stare her mother down. Then, hating herself for not being brave enough to walk out the front door and slam it behind her, she stomped up the stairs.

CHAPTER FOURTEEN

THREE AGONIZING DAYS LATER, IN THE MIDST OF ALL THE preparations for the final show, Raven convinced Flint to meet her outside Delphinium College during her lunch break.

"She made you choose?" he asked.

"Yes. Although I didn't actually choose, of course, since I'm seeing you now and I don't plan to give you up. It's so silly. Once graduation is done, I can leave then. Didn't she consider that?"

"I'm sure she did. She's probably hoping she'll convince you otherwise between now and then."

"Well she won't. If I get the internship, I'll be able to support myself. And if I don't … well, I'll figure something out."

They stood next to each other, leaning against one of the

trees, Flint's hand clasped around Raven's.

"I went to the Guild," he said.

"Oh yeah?"

"They're happy for me to work there again."

"That's great. I'm so glad to hear that my mother hasn't completely ruined your career for you."

"She tried," Flint said with a grim smile, "but I explained my side of the story, and fortunately there are people at the Guild who are sensible enough to see that what happened with you and me isn't something that will affect the work I do for the Guild."

"Good. So I just need to get through the final show tomorrow, and everything should be okay after that."

Flint let go of her hand and moved to stand in front of her. He didn't smile, and he hesitated for far too long, and suddenly she knew exactly where this was going.

"Don't," she said before he could speak. "Don't end this. My parents are an obstacle we can get past."

He shook his head. "They're not. And they shouldn't have to be."

"Then I'll make them see what I see. That you're amazing, and worth far more than any spoiled rich boy they want to pair me with."

"Raven." He sighed. "I care a great deal about you. Probably far more than you know. And I want you to fight for me, but I don't want you to have to fight your parents."

"But I—"

"I won't let you choose between me and your family. It isn't right, and you'll end up hating me for it."

"What about what I want? What if I'm happy to choose? I know I could never hate you."

She wrapped her arms around her chest and stared through a sheen of tears at the ground. "Does it matter at all to you that you're breaking my heart?"

"Raven ..."

"I hope you know that you aren't just ending a brief romance that started a few days ago. You're ending something so much deeper. Every conversation, every laugh, every dream. All the day-to-day things we shared. Why does that have to be less important than the rocky relationship I have with my parents? Why don't you believe me when I say I'd rather choose you?"

"Because ... because I think you'll grow to regret it."

She pressed her lips together, swallowed her tears, and looked past him. "Then you don't know me at all."

"Raven, I ... I'm sorry. I didn't mean for this to happen the day before your big show."

"Just go. Actually, I'll go. Lunch is almost over anyway."

"Raven—"

"Goodbye."

CHAPTER FIFTEEN

It hurt more than Raven thought possible. She almost didn't get out of bed the next morning. Then she reminded herself that maybe, possibly, *somehow* she wouldn't always have a broken heart, and when that day came, she would want to know she'd done everything possible to win the House of Cascata internship. Besides, she was proud of her collection; she wanted everyone to see it.

She lost herself in the flurry of activity surrounding the show. Models, makeup, hair stylists, clothes hovering all over the place, and accessories spinning around. It was the kind of chaos she enjoyed. As the start of the show grew rapidly closer, she fussed around her models, checking the finer details of their outfits, and sending them back to hair or makeup if something hadn't been done to her exact specifications.

"Madeline, where are your gloves?" she asked one of the girls. "The luminescent ones."

"Oh, that's right. There were gloves. I haven't seen them since the last fitting."

Biting down on her frustration, Raven returned to the storeroom and walked to her section. The gloves lay on the floor. She quickly drew her pattern code in the air with her stylus, stepped inside the space, and picked up the gloves. She took one step out before swinging back around. Her storage section was empty. Completely empty.

Where was the sprite-wing dress?

She asked everyone she passed on her way back, but no one had seen it. *Why?* she demanded silently. Why would someone take it? No one else could use it now. Everyone knew she was the one who'd made it. But she pushed her questions to the back of her mind. She'd have to figure out where the dress had gone later.

She handed Madeline her gloves and bent down to adjust the fish scales at the bottom of her dress.

"Hey, did you see all the guardians outside and in the hallways?" It was Poe, obviously finished getting his models ready. "They must be worried about another explosion."

"Um, some of them, I guess."

"I saw your handsome bodyguard out there."

"Oh, really?" Raven looked up in surprise.

"Yes." Poe frowned. "Why wouldn't he be here? Isn't he supposed to go everywhere with you?"

Raven looked down again. "He, uh, isn't working for my parents anymore. He's with the Creepy Hollow Guild now."

He must have been assigned here tonight as part of the extra security. Or perhaps, she thought with a traitorous lurch of her heart, he'd volunteered. So he could see her.

Stop it, she told herself. Flint had made it clear things weren't going to work out for the two of them.

"Five minutes until we start!" Poe said with a squeal, clutching Raven's arm as she stood.

"Your collection is first, right?" she asked.

"Yes. Yours?"

"Third.

"Ohmygosh I'm so nervous," Jessima said, running up to both of them. "I can't believe we've finally reached this point."

"I know," Raven said. "It doesn't quite feel real." She wished she could peek beyond the curtains at the packed auditorium. Her parents were out there, despite the fact that she'd barely spoken to them in days, and so was Daisy. Daisy's final design work had been judged the afternoon before, so the only thing she still had to get through was graduation the next afternoon.

Raven tried to breathe past her nervousness, her eyes skimming over her models for any last imperfections. "Wait, where's Cass?" she asked, referring to the model wearing her final piece, the snake dress.

"Uh, she was here just now," someone said.

"Ugh, why can't everyone stay where they're supposed to be?" Raven complained. She asked around, and someone said he'd seen Cass near the stairs leading above the stage. "Where the special effects enchantments are controlled?" she asked.

"Yeah. She was with Cecilia."

Confused, Raven hurried toward the stairs. There were a few special effects she'd discussed with Cecilia, but all instructions had already been passed on to the relevant people. Had Cecilia decided to change something? If she had, it could only be for the better, but surely she didn't need to take one of Raven's models with her when the show was about to begin?

She ran up the stairs as quickly as her heels would allow. The large space above the auditorium was dimly lit, but there was almost as much activity happening up here as downstairs. No models or fancy clothes, but plenty of people hurrying around and others sitting beside circular holes in the floor that obviously gave them a view of the stage and runway below. Holes that must be invisible from the auditorium, since Raven had never seen them before.

Her eyes scanned the area, but she couldn't find Cecilia or Cass. This space was only about half the size of the auditorium, though, which must mean there were other places to go up here. She grabbed someone's arm, pointed to a narrow passageway running along the side of the far wall, and asked, "Are there rooms or something down there?"

"Yes, for storage. Props and things."

"Thanks." That must be what Cecilia was after. Some kind of prop she'd decided would go well with the snake dress.

Slightly muffled, but still audible, the welcome music began to play. "Crap," Raven muttered. The show was starting, and she needed her last model. She ran to the passage and pushed open door after door. Every room was dark, though, until—

"Oh, I'm so glad I found you," she said as she stumbled

into the next room and saw Cecilia. Then her eyes fell upon a girl she didn't recognize—wearing her fully repaired sprite-wing dress and headpiece—and then Cass, crumpled on the floor.

Without warning, the door swung shut behind Raven.

CHAPTER SIXTEEN

"WHAT—WHAT HAPPENED TO CASS?" RAVEN LOWERED herself to the floor beside the model. She was still breathing, but showed no sign of waking. "Cecilia?" Raven looked up, suspicion crowding her senses. "What's going on?"

"Raven, finally. I was worried you weren't going to show up. Don't worry about Cass. She'll be fine when she wakes, though she won't remember anything. She was just the bait to get you here."

"Bait?" Raven stood. "Jeez, Cecilia. You could have sent me a message."

"What, and have you ignore me like last time? You probably don't even know where your amber is in all this mayhem."

"Last time? Did you ... were you the one who sent that

weird message about escaping death and making the most of the rest of my life?"

"Yes." Cecilia leaned against a stack of chairs. "I need you on my side, Raven, so I was hoping to warm you up to my ideas beforehand. I thought you might be open to them, having just been rejected by the director and then narrowly escaping death, but I realized you probably wouldn't have agreed with *everything* I want to do. You might have tried to stop me, so it was better to wait until now and force your hand."

"Force my—"

"Obviously I don't *want* to force you into anything. It would be better if you cooperate."

"Stop. Hold on." Raven held one hand up, palm facing Cecilia. "You've stolen my dress, knocked out my model, probably caused that explosion two weeks ago, and now you want me to cooperate with you on something? Cecilia, are you okay? This all just seems exceedingly strange."

Cecilia smiled. "I'm okay. At least, I will be soon. Once I've killed my sister."

Raven's eyes widened as her mouth dropped open. She looked at the girl wearing her sprite dress—a girl who seemed quite bored—then back at Cecilia. "You are definitely not okay." She reached behind her for the door handle. "Why don't I go fetch one of the other teachers." She twisted it, but the door wouldn't open.

"I can't let you go until I know you're on my side, Raven. Just hear me out."

Instead of answering, Raven pressed her back against the

door. Hopefully she could figure out the right spell to open it while Cecilia was talking.

"My sister doesn't deserve to be the head of the House of Cascata," Cecilia said. "That position should always have been mine, and it's time I claim it for myself."

"Wait, Mella Cascata is your sister?"

"Yes. Sorry, I forgot you didn't know that. She always called me the ugly one, which is why I was so pleasantly surprised the other day when you said I look like her."

"Why don't we all know that she's your sister?"

"Same reason you don't know that Mella Cascata has two brothers, or that her uncle is a halfling, or that her father died of a drug overdose: she distanced herself from her family years ago. But she and I came up with the House of Cascata idea while we were still teens, training as clothes casters. Decades later, after paying me off to stay away so she wouldn't be threatened by my talent, she's the queen of fashion and I'm just a teacher."

"And now you want to kill her?"

Cecilia sighed. She played with the end of a peacock feather sticking out past a lamp. "I'm not a bad person, Raven. You know that. I've simply been dealt a bad hand. I thought I could put up with it, being shoved aside as the unskilled sister while she took credit for dozens of my early designs, but after ... after last month when I ..." Her voice wobbled. She took a deep breath and focused on the floor. "Mella and I began meeting again recently. I wanted to patch things up. Perhaps leave Delph and find a way to work with her at the House of Cascata. But then I discovered that—that she and my ... my *husband* had been—" She cut herself off and shook her head. "For months. *Months.* And after the way she treated me before, I just couldn't take this. The betrayal, the humiliation. She might have had the illustrious career, but I've always had *him.* That was enough for me. But then to find out that she took him too? No. She doesn't deserve anything now. Not a single thing."

"I'm sorry, Cecilia," Raven said carefully. "That's awful. But ... killing your sister won't make you feel any better."

Cecilia sniffed and dried her eyes. "Of course it will. And it's your dress that's going to do the job."

"What?"

"Don't worry, I've got it all worked out. I changed the records so that it looks like Director Drizwold did approve your dress. We'll lower the model down from here—" she rolled Cass's unconscious body over so that Raven could see another one of those circular holes in the floor "—and it will seem as though it's part of the show. Since the dress has wings, it'll work perfectly. When she reaches the end of the runway and the fire spells—which haven't been fixed—ignite, she'll pull off the headpiece just like you did, and throw it at Mella. Of course, it will look like an accident. A model panicking and saving herself. Then my sister will be killed by the explosion, and in a few weeks or months, when everything is settled, I will step up to take over the House of Cascata."

Raven almost laughed out loud at this ridiculous plan. "But there'll be an investigation, and the director will say she *didn't* approve the outfit. And what about all the other students who know that my dress wasn't approved?"

"Director Drizwold is sitting right next to Mella. She probably won't survive the explosion. And the other students ..." Cecilia waved her hand in dismissal. "It will all work out. No one believes what students say."

Raven was convinced by now that Cecilia wasn't entirely in her right mind. "And what about me? *I* will tell the Guild everything that's happened. You could try to kill me too, I guess, but you said just now that you need me on your side."

"Well I don't *need* you, but I'd like you to be there. Your designs are only going to get better and better, and together the two of us could ensure the House of Cascata remains at the top of the fashion pyramid forever. Just think about it. This is the best opportunity you're ever going to get."

The model in the sprite dress leaned forward to look down the hole. "Raven's first model just came on."

Raven had the sudden urge to start crying. This was her moment—her *final show*—and she was missing it because her favorite teacher had turned into a vengeful nutcase. "What if I say no to this amazing opportunity you're offering me?"

"Unfortunately, your parents will then suffer the consequences." Cecilia knelt down and waved her hand across the hole. The semi-transparent glass that had sealed it vanished, and the music abruptly grew louder. Raven's music. Music she'd spent hours choosing. "You see," Cecilia continued as she straightened, "I've been gathering funds for a few months now. Funds for a children's charity—or so I told the generous donors. In reality, the money has gone to a service that will ensure a fake version of Mella's will winds up in the right hands. A fake version that will leave everything to me. Oh, and your parents happen to be the only donors. So if you decide to tell the Guild what I've done, your parents will go down with me."

"I'll bet they're the only donors because they're the only people you asked." Raven angrily balled her hands into fists. "Just so you'd have something to blackmail me with. You really have gone crazy."

"I don't think so." Cecilia pulled her model closer and helped her to sit at the edge of the circle. "I think *you* might be crazy if you don't see the obvious benefits of this plan."

"All I can see are the obvious *holes*. You can't get away with this, Cecilia."

"Yes I can. And I'm about to start now." She pushed the girl off the edge.

"Wait, no!" Raven dashed to the edge of the circle, but the girl was descending slowly, gracefully, instead of plummeting down onto the runway as Raven had feared. "You didn't give me any time to think."

"What's there to think about?" Cecilia asked. "Would you really bring complete ruin to your family by exposing the illegal activity your parents have been involved in?"

"They didn't know what they were doing."

"Doesn't make it any less illegal."

"Cecilia, you have to stop this," Raven pleaded, growing more desperate. "You can't *kill* people." If Cecilia brought this plan to a halt, Raven wouldn't have to stop it herself and reveal her parents' involvement. She might disagree with them about a great many things, but she didn't want to ruin their lives. She loved them.

"I'm not stopping anything." Cecilia closed the hole and stood over it. "Raven, just let this happen. You don't even have to watch it. It'll end up being a tragic accident. People might blame you for a while, but the House of Cascata will become stronger than ever, everyone will remember that Mella was actually a horrible person, and I'll restore your name by showing you forgiveness and extending an invitation to work with me."

Raven said nothing. Her heart pounded painfully fast as she ran through every move Flint had shown her. Unfortunately, it had been some time since she practiced anything, and she was sure that absolutely nothing would come instinctively to her.

But she was out of time, so she threw herself at Cecilia and hoped for the best. The two of them tumbled into the stack of chairs. They fell onto Cass, then rolled over the hole. Raven pushed sparks out from her hand—formless and directionless, but sparks nonetheless—and Cecilia cried out as her cheek burned. Raven's hand moved down to the glass circle. *Come on, magic, come on.* What would work? A pulse? Heat? Kicking the darn thing? "Come on!" she yelled, and a shockwave of power finally released itself from her hand just as Cecilia tore at her face.

She cried out and jerked away. Cecilia pushed her off. They both managed to scramble to their feet, and that was when Raven noticed the large crack across the glass circle. She ran and jumped—and with a splintering crack, the floor gave way.

They both screamed as they fell. *Stop, stop, stop!* Raven's brain shrieked at her, and her magic cushioned and dropped her just inches above the runway. Cecilia landed with a heavy thump beside her. She barely moved.

Screams erupted all around them. Raven pushed herself up and looked toward the end of the runway. The sprite-wing dress was already on fire. She clambered up and ran faster than she'd ever thought possible in a pair of heels. The model pulled the flaming headpiece off. She raised her hand, pulled it back—and Raven grabbed the headpiece from her. She couldn't stop herself in time, so she ended up toppling off the end of the runway and landing in the laps of those in the first row: Mella, Director Drizwold, and everyone else she'd been hoping to save.

They gasped and shrieked and pushed her away—which was exactly what she needed. She got onto her feet, and with all her might, tossed the metal headpiece back toward the stage. It sailed over the model, over Cecilia, and exploded in midair.

* * *

In the aftermath, with smoke rising from the stage, guardians and healers moving about, and injured guests crying out, Raven stood with her mother and father on either side of her and finished telling the guardian with the tiny notepad everything she could remember—except her parents' supposed involvement. When she was done, the guardian briefly explained what would happen next, something about an investigation and further questioning, probably under the influence of compulsion potion to make sure her story was true. He continued speaking, but Raven was overcome with tiredness and all his words began to blend together.

She looked behind him and saw Flint. He was speaking to one of the teachers. He pointed to the stage, the teacher nodded, and he wrote something down. The teacher nodded and walked away. Then Flint looked up, across the auditorium, and straight at Raven. She wished she could smile at him, but it seemed like far too much of an effort right now. Then her mother tucked her against her side and steered her away toward the door.

CHAPTER SEVENTEEN

"Is it finally over?" Poe asked.

Raven dropped onto the couch beside him in his parents' living room. "It's finally over." It was one month and one day since the disastrous final show at Delphinium College, and the Guild had finally finished dealing with the resulting mess. "A month isn't all that long if you think about it," she said.

"I supposed it isn't. I'm so glad we have magic to assist with stuff like this. I hear these things take forever in the human world."

"Yeah. Hey, have you seen my green dress with the glowing polka dots? I'm sure I unpacked it into the closet in the guest room, but I couldn't find it this morning."

"You mean the closet that's perpetually open on the bedroom floor?"

She rolled her eyes. "It isn't *that* bad."

"It is that bad. Do you dump *everything* you wear on the floor?"

She sighed and pushed herself to her feet. "Okay, I'll go tidy it up. Want to help me?"

"Not really. I'll sit on the bed and watch you."

They traipsed up the stairs together. Raven had moved out of her parents' home several days after the final show. She, Zalea and Kenrick had had plenty of things to argue about before she made her decision to leave: Flint, her failed career, the scandalous revelation that her parents had somehow been funding a fashion school teacher who'd gone crazy and tried to murder people. Raven hadn't cared if she'd left with only the clothes she was wearing. All she knew was that she needed to get away.

She went to Daisy's first, but Daisy's mom had made it clear that the girl involved in almost blowing up the Delphinium College auditorium wasn't welcome in her home. Poe, a former scholarship student whose parents didn't move in the same circles as hers or Daisy's, had been happy to take her in for a little while. Poe's house was very much like Flint's, and Raven couldn't help thinking of him often. Actually, she could have been surrounded by anything and her thoughts would still have turned to Flint. She missed him terribly.

"So what did the Guild decide about your parents?" Poe asked as he jumped onto the bed in the room that used to belong to his older sister. Raven perched on the edge and picked up clothes with continuous flicks of her hand, sending them into two piles in the corner: clean and dirty.

"The charges against them were dropped. My dad obviously had paperwork that proved he was donating money to a charity. Or *thought* he was donating money to a charity. So everything's okay. With all the people interviewed under the influence of compulsion potion, the real story couldn't help but come out."

"Cool. And Cecilia? Did they decide she's crazy after all?"

"Yes. They sent her off to a home for mentally unstable fae. Anyway, how was your day? Was Mella in a better mood?"

"Ugh, is she *ever* in any form of good mood?" Poe draped himself dramatically across the cushions on the bed. "I don't think so. I was shouted at even more today than yesterday."

Poe had come top of the class and won the Cascata internship. Raven hadn't even placed in the top three. "Poor Poe," she said without a hint of sympathy. "The price of success is high."

He sat up and threw a cushion at her. She caught it and was about to toss it back when the door knocker on the outside of the tree banged three times. "Expecting someone?" Poe asked.

"Nope. You?"

He shook his head. They walked back downstairs and Poe headed for the section of the wall where a doorway could be opened. He drew a tiny peephole on the wall with his stylus and looked through it. "It's a guy with a good-looking top hat," he said before writing a doorway spell.

A space appeared in the wall, revealing a rotund man with an impressive top hat. He had to bend slightly to come inside. "Good afternoon. Is Raven Rosewood here?"

"Uh, that's me." Raven walked forward, feeling a little

bewildered. The man seemed familiar, but she couldn't place him.

"Miss Rosewood," he said. "My name is Mr. Von Milta. Perhaps you don't remember me, but I run the Von Milta Madness event. We displayed some of your work this year and auctioned it off quite successfully."

"Oh, yes. I do remember you."

"I heard that the spectacular dress explosion at Delphinium College was your creation."

"Oh. Yes." Disappointment clouded over her once again. Was she never going to live this down? "I was responsible for that, although it was never my intention to use the outfit for—"

"I know, I know, don't worry about that." He waved her words away. "I'm not here to blame you for anything. On the contrary. We've been waiting for the whole matter to be cleared up by the Guild before extending an offer to you. We received word this morning that the investigation or the case—cases?—or whatever it is they call these things is finished."

"Yes, that's correct. Wait, did you say 'offer'?"

"I did indeed." Mr. Von Milta beamed at her. "We have dozens of projects going on throughout the year. Some for charity, the occasional celebrity event, projects with faerie junior schools, and plenty more. We'd love for you to be part of our creative department."

"I—oh—wow."

"I have the offer right here." He held up a scroll. "No need to respond right now. Take a few days, read it over, think about it. If you have any questions, let me know. Then we can take it from there."

"Um, okay." She took the scroll from him, wondering if she might possibly be dreaming.

"Well, good day then." Mr. Von Milta tipped his hat, turned around, and left the house.

Raven blinked at the scroll in her hand. She looked up at Poe, and together they started laughing.

CHAPTER EIGHTEEN

"THIS WAY, THIS WAY," RAVEN CALLED TO THE LINE OF children leaving the unicorn-themed play park. "Nope, not that way." She ran after a boy who'd been distracted by a string of bubbles floating past him and veered off course. She took his hand and led him to the back of the line, glancing up to make sure her colleague Ennie was still at the front.

"Are you new?" the boy asked. "I don't remember you from last time."

Raven looked down at him as she answered. "Yes, I'm brand new. I've only been here three weeks."

"So you get to come here every day?"

"I do."

"You're really lucky." His shoulders drooped and his lips turned down. "I wish I could come here every day."

"Hey, if you came every day, it wouldn't be that fun. This way you have something to look forward to."

The boy frowned, as though he wasn't sure he agreed with her.

Raven walked with the children back through the Von Milta Building to the door their teachers were waiting at. "Hey, Raven, I just got back." Maria, another one of her coworkers, ran toward her. "I can take over from here if you want."

"Thanks." Raven removed a clipboard from beneath her arm and handed it over. "Sheesh, they're a handful. I'm glad I work behind the scenes most days."

Maria smiled. "Yeah, they're crazy, but I love them. Oh, there's someone waiting for you at reception."

"Okay, thanks. Skinny guy, lots of piercings?"

She laughed and shook her head. "Not even close."

Raven took the shortcut to reception: straight down the pole to the ground level. She walked toward the main desk, shaped like a top hat, and saw—

Flint.

Her stomach flipped over and her heart leaped into her throat. A surge of magic escaped her hands in the form of glitter-filled bubbles. She forced both hands behind her back. "Hi, Flint," she said as she walked up to him.

He turned, dropped something on the floor, and bent quickly to pick it up. "Hi. Sorry. Hello." He smiled. "It's really nice to see you, Raven."

She took a deep breath and nodded. "It's nice to see you too."

"I, uh, have something of yours that I never returned." He held the something out toward her. It was her notebook with the sample of Cecilia's handwriting. She'd given it to him to take to the Guild.

She started laughing as she took it. "Really? You wanted to return my notebook? Surely you could have come up with a better excuse than that."

Color appeared in his cheeks. He looked down, then back up at her. "To be honest, I had a whole list of potential excuses, but they all seemed equally transparent. This one was the most legitimate, since I thought you might actually want to keep the sketches inside this notebook." He lifted one shoulder. "I just ... wanted to see how you're doing."

"I'm doing very well, actually." She moved away from the top-hat desk, feeling weird having this conversation right next to the person sitting behind it. Flint followed her. "I like it here," she added, turning to face him again. "It isn't what I hoped for while studying at Delph, but I think that's a good thing. It's a lot more rewarding than dressing celebrities all day."

"I can imagine. Do you miss the clothes casting though?"

"Not too much. I get to do some of it here and there. But for now I'm enjoying exploring different creative forms." She pushed her hands into the pockets of her striped shorts. "I'll save up, and maybe one day I'll start my own business, or just hire out my skills as a clothes caster. I don't know. I guess I'll see where life takes me. How's it going at the Guild?"

"I'm enjoying being back there. It's challenging at times, but in a good way."

She nodded, and they stood in silence for a few moments.

"How are your parents doing?" Flint asked.

"Um, they're okay. Still recovering from the scandal of being associated with the crazy fashion school teacher who tried to blow up Mella Cascata. We, uh, didn't talk for a while. But we're slowly patching things up now. Working toward a mutual understanding and respect of each other's priorities."

"Must be interesting going through all that under the same roof," Flint said. "Although having a large house probably helps. You don't have much chance of bumping into each other."

"Oh, no, I don't live there anymore. I stayed with Poe for a while, and then after I started working here, I moved upstairs. They have accommodation for employees."

"Oh, cool." He hesitated, looked down at his hands, then tucked them both behind his back. "Raven, I'm really sorry for the way I ended things before. I didn't want to create a divide between you and your parents, but I should have trusted that together we could get them to accept ... us."

"It's fine, really," she said. "I understand where you were coming from. Especially having lost your dad. Family's hugely important to you, and it was good that you reminded me of that. It's important to me too. I'm working hard on maintaining a relationship with my parents, even though they're not the easiest people."

"Well, anyway, I still shouldn't have hurt you like that."

She shook her head and smiled. "It's in the past."

He let out a breath he might possibly have been holding

since he walked in here. "Okay, well, it was great talking to you. I should probably go."

"Okay."

He turned away, then swung back around to face her. "Do you want to get a drink sometime? Or dinner or something?"

A smile spread across her face. "I do, yes."

"Tonight?"

"Tonight works well."

"Great." He took another step away, then turned to face her yet again. "I missed you. A lot. You can probably tell."

She chuckled and nodded. She rocked forward onto her toes, then back down again. "Can you tell how much I missed you?"

"Uh ... not really."

She didn't pause. A moment later, her arms were around his neck, and she was hugging him tightly. "Can you tell now?"

His arms came up around her back and pulled her closer. He nodded against her hair. "Yes."

They stood like that for quite some time before she pressed a brief kiss to his neck and stepped back. "I'll see you tonight?"

"Yes. I'm very much looking forward to it."

She smiled. "Me too."

Find out how Raven and Flint fit into the main series of Creepy Hollow novels by starting with *The Faerie Guardian*.

www.creepyhollowbooks.com

Rachel Morgan spent a good deal of her childhood living
in a fantasy land of her own making, crafting endless stories of
make-believe and occasionally writing some of them down.
After completing a degree in genetics and discovering
she still wasn't grown-up enough for a 'real' job, she decided
to return to those story worlds still spinning around her
imagination. These days she spends much of her time
immersed in fantasy land once more, writing fiction
for young adults and those young at heart.

Rachel lives in Cape Town with her husband and
three miniature dachshunds. She is the author of the
bestselling Creepy Hollow series and the sweet
contemporary romance Trouble series.

www.rachel-morgan.com